911
IN
THE
HOOD

MELISSA COBB

Moral Statement

"Beware of the advice you give."

Dedication

To the Hood above all Hoods, JTM.

(Jamestown Mafia)

Changing the Heart
presents

911 in the Hood

A Novel by
Melissa Cobb

Chapter 1

My Creative Writing teacher spoke to the class about raising the bar. He said, "We are lucky to be the person we are and to have the family we have in our life."

Turning my head, I thought *if he thinks calling your uncle daddy, fucking everything in the hood, and living from house to house before moving to Billy Goat Hill lucky, I guess I would be a lucky ass bitch.* Before I could indulge more, the bell rang. I walked out of the classroom to see a group of people. Walking closer to the huddle, in the middle was my girl, my vindictive bitch, Party.

She said to La-La, "I did your stank ass a favor, plus, your man can't fuck. Since y'all broke up, you didn't have to worry about pleasing him. I took your slack."

"You country talking bitch, you fucked my man? I mean, your trifling, free fuck ass fucked my man? My man!"

"That's what I said, you city talking, uppity ass bitch. Did… did… did… did I stutter? If you see a bitch, you…" Before Party could open her mouth to say another word, La-La punched her in her mouth. Blood gushed out everywhere, but that didn't stop the two. The fight was on and popping.

"Bust that bitch in the head. Let's see her red shit," I yelled at Party.

As every fist connected to skin, I could hear the hits like

someone kicking against the wall. They were standing toe to toe, fighting like two grown ass men.

"Whip that ass, Party, get that out of state bitch!" a boy screamed out in the crowd as he jumped up and down in full excitement.

"Don't kill her, but make that bitch suffer. She talked about Mississippi too damn much. Bust that ass!" another person yelled out.

The crowd was going wild as they yelled and screamed. I looked on as they fought, and then suddenly La-La body slammed Party to the ground hard. The crowd said in unison, "Ooh!"

La-La, without hesitation, jumped on top of my girl and punched her in the face repeatedly. I got angry because those punches were harsh to grasp, and I was on the outside looking in. To encourage Party, I screamed over the crowd, "Get the fuck up, Party! What the fuck you doing? Fighting on your ass?"

"Get up, get up!" the people began to chant. Party looked as if she was tired as hell as she tried to hold the girl closer to stop her connecting fists.

However, I got even closer to wait for the cue. Party said with her eyes, "Get this bitch off me."

That was all I needed. La-La was still going strong like a motherfucker. I must admit, Party was hanging in. That bitch was banging like she was on some new shit. Without warning, I punched La-La on the right side of her face and her body fell over like a limp noodle before realization kicked in. That time frame was enough for Party to jump up and straddled La-La in her familiar stance. Now, it is Party whom was taking control and beating that ass like she stole something.

Suddenly, someone grabbed me and slung me back. Turning around to look, it was that other bitch from Memphis.

"What the fuck is up with you? Don't you ever put your damn hands on me again!" I yelled in her face to get her in check.

"You need to stay the hell out this fight," she replied with much attitude.

"Trick, you must have forgotten who I am."

"Yeah, I know who you are and to be honest, I don't give two flying fucks. Let it be one on one. If ya girl getting her ass kicked, let my girl kick that ass," she spoke as she pushed me.

I dropped my book bag so fast and punched her in her jaw. She fell towards the ground. Before anything could become more of it, teachers rushed in and broke everything up. Party, La-La, the chick I didn't know, and I were carried to the office for fighting. We all got three days at home like we gave a shit about it. That was where we wanted to be, anyway.

Smiling back on the day's memory as we went towards

home, I must admit that it was wild. The principal and teachers were probably happy it was our last year. I was just as glad as they are. They had no idea how much of a full-time job it was to be me and keep Party in school.

To kick things off, my name is Mahogany, but people in the hood called me "Hog." I'm eighteen years old with a caramel complexion, brown eyes, and Coke bottle shape. Yes, and a nice round ass. I'm sexy as hell. Anyway, let me tell you about my family and share with you how the fire got started at 911-In the Hood...

Our family was down for whatever and whoever. If you stepped to us the wrong way, we would handle you the wrong way. And, if Patricia, aka Party and I were not enough, her brothers, my favorite cousins, Bone and Rabbit, would be because they ran the hood and every shit in it. Besides, The Hill was known from Jackson and surpassed Sebastopol. No one fucked with us.

Party is also eighteen years old. She was shorter, rounder and darker with a big mouth and lots of attitude to go along with the looks. Her shoulders were kind of broad, but she had a big swing in her hips to throw her big ass all over the place. My girl knew her shit, which was why Party was the bomb when it came to fucking up your home and partying. Her smooth tongue could sell you a car with no motor and before you knew it, you would be hustled, home-wrecked, and out on the street. She was just that good.

I smiled at that thought because we were close. As for

Party, I would not trade anything for her because I loved her and hated her at the same time. How often did a ride or die bitch come into your life and be kin to you? Not often was the answer because we believed in family and sticking up for family. If the family didn't stand by you, no one else would was what we believe.

Pandora, known as Pan, who was my mom, and Terri aka Aunt Tee, who is my cousins' mother, were sisters, and we all live on The Hill. Nothing ever happened without us being involved and no matter where we went everyone knew of The Hill. Yes, the name was very unique. Our address was 911 Billy Bay Drive, but we ended up being called 911 Billy Goat Hill. It was crazy how we got that name.

It started with, Bone, aka Bart, and Peter aka Rabbit, raised Billy goats. Boys from the hood, along with Bone and Rabbit, used to go out and fight the goats until they held them down and snapped their necks. Many people would come out and watch them wrestle with the goats until they were busted by the animal cruelty people. Every Saturday they put the goats on the grill and served up the hood. There was nothing like a good, barbecued goat.

My mind was still wrapped on my Creative Writing teacher's words. He talked about life outside of the one we know. On the way home, I mentioned it to my girl, but she only threw in my face about me thinking I was smart; therefore, I changed the subject.

When we made it home, we decided to go down the

road. I began to laugh to myself as I spoke to Party while walking. "Girl, I just thought about something."

"What's so funny?" Party asked.

"Do you remember when that Memphis bitch jumped you today?" I spoke.

"Hell yeah, I had that ass beat and here you come, wanting in by hitting La-La," Party spoke as we walked.

"Well, if you were on top and not on the bottom, I wouldn't have punched her ass up off you. You did give me the sign," I remarked.

"Ouch. Fuck that. You know I was beating her city talking ass."

"Yeah, on the bottom," I joked as Party hit me on the arm in jester.

We became engrossed in thoughts, for we were no longer the children we used to be, but becoming grown women in this dog-eat-dog ass world. It had never occurred to me about what I wanted to do for books, hanging under the tree and being with Party was all I had ever done. I guess it went back to our elementary days.

Our mothers dressed us alike every day until middle school, and that was when people finally realized we weren't twins. She had her own style, and I had mine, but I was always behind whatever Party wanted to do. Yeah, I was a follower. We got our ass beat together and we fought together. It was whatever when it came down to Party and me.

We continued to walk down the dirt road to Aunt Doll's house. Her real name is Darlene, and she is our mothers' baby sister. Party's dad was the whore- the family heirloom. It was fucked up because he was with my mom first, and then he moved on to Party's mom, and now he was with Aunt Doll. They are sisters sharing a piece of dick, with few complaints; what a life.

Oddly enough, I was smart and had scholarships lined up, but they didn't give out degrees for what I really know, which was pimping bitches and tricking motherfuckers. From being in the hood, you had to have a hood mentality to survive. Despite the drama we got into, I was always the levelheaded one and Party was the hit now talk later kind of girl. Glancing at Party, she walked without saying a word. So, I decided to speak up again about what I said on the way home.

"My thoughts are really bothering me about what my Creative Writing teacher spoke. Have you wondered about life outside of the hood? He wanted to know what I was going to do with my life after I graduate."

After allowing the notion, again, to linger that we could do better after high school, Party said, "Yeah, what are you going to do?"

"Nothing, girl, I'll probably be right here in the hood doing what I know how to do and that is tricking niggas and making that money," I joked as I held up my hand for a high five from Party as we laughed it off. "But I have had it with these tired ass niggas around here. You know it is the same dick, but with a different excuse. What about you?"

"As if you didn't know, bitch, I'm going to be harder than my daddy and hustle like my momma. There is money out here to be made and I plan to make sure I get my share," Party replied.

"Shit, there isn't anything wrong with that if that is what you want to do; have to get your name out there. You already on your way just wish you would go to school," I replied.

"It's not just me getting my name out there and going to school, it's us getting our names out there. I'm not going to leave you behind; you're the fucking brains of my entire operations. I have to keep your ass on my team. You feel me?" Party told me.

"True. I am the brains," I replied as I laughed.

"I need to stop fucking all these broke asses, wanna be niggas and go after some real cake. Like Cousin Po Boy," Party replied as we walked pass his house.

Cousin Po Boy was one of our great aunt's only child. He didn't hang out with his family, but deep down he was just as dirty as he want to be. He was a lanky, dark-skinned brother with three gold teeth on the right side and he had mad money. All the broke bitches in the hood were after that nigga, cousin or not.

"Yeah, he does look good with that new Mercedes and Hummer. I wonder if his wife is happy," I replied.

"Hell no. He doesn't want her sorry ass. That's why he is sweating me like a hound and after this young, tender pussy" Party said as we laughed hard. He looked up at us and we waved hello as we walked past him standing in his long driveway.

"No matter the time of day, he always finds his way to be here when we walk by. Have you noticed it?" Party asked.

"I have but thought it was by chance. I see the way he watches us when we walk up and down the road. He acts like he is better than us. I guess he is waiting on us to come on to him."

"He starts showing me some Franklins and he can have this pussy. Money doesn't have a face and for the right price, he won't have one, either. The problem is can he handle this hot piece of ass?" Party questioned as we walked further down the road laughing.

"What about his wife?" I asked.

"What about her? She can't do shit for me but shut the fuck up and let her husband give me some of that damn money he steals from people," Party said.

The laughter was short lived. When we made it by the big ditch, I was about to go to the right and Party to the left until we saw Aunt Doll and Don going at it.

"You punk ass bitch, you fucking everybody and then

want to give me your tired ass dick. What the fuck! This is my motherfucking house and my damn truck. I work to pay the bills here. You and my brother just live at this bitch. You maggot fuckers don't contribute shit but sit around here and nag like a damn fly on shit. How the hell can I bum if y'all bumming off me and pulling me down? I can't keep putting up with this shit. I own this shit and every damn thing here. That includes your ass, too. You my shit and if you don't like it, you can get your rags and get the fuck on, bitch. I can be finished with you," Aunt Doll screamed like a wildcat.

"Shit, you know what the fuck is up. You act like this shit brand new to you. Doll, you were not born yesterday. You knew I was a dog when you started fucking off with me. I was fucking your sisters first; I just ran across your ass on accident. Shit, we both fucking every motherfucking body up and down the neighborhood, so why the hell you tripping now? You say you work, bitch work the motherfucking streets," Don said as he was amused at her anger.

"You trick off with those Gutta Sluts, those nasty ass bitches. You give them the good dick," Aunt Doll said angrily.

The Gutta Sluts are our cousins that lived across the street from Party and me but down a long dirt road. They were two fat sisters, and the hood called them Yogi and Pinky. Those hood bitches had dick on top of dick on lock, and they were cool ass bitches even though they fucked for free half the time.

"How else do you think I pay for your hair, nails, and other shit when your pussy doesn't pay off? Yeah, by tricking off with those nasty bitches for their shit and I do what? I bring their nasty, trick ass money to you. Don't I, baby girl?" Don said with a smile as he reached for Aunt Doll.

"You no good motherfucker," Aunt Doll said as she stood in his face as if she wanted to hit him.

"Say what the fuck you want. I need to go up there now to slide this dick in a throat to get me some real action. Shit, that pussy stank half the time and the rest of the time it's bleeding. Now your ass tell me, who tired?" Don said with a smile as he feasted off his hurling words to her.

"You know what, get the fuck out. Take your tired ass to one of those bitches and let them take care of you," Aunt Doll said as she continued to hit on Don while everyone watched outside in the yard.

"That ain't nothing but a thang, Doll. Shit, you know me, I don't give a fuck," Don said.

Aunt Doll went in the house and walked back outside. When she returned, she threw his grocery bag of clothes and freshly pressed clothes on the hanger at him. They all fell on the ground.

"Damn, Doll, what the fuck you doing? Is this what you really want? Bitch, is this really what the fuck you want? Aight bet that up!" Don asked slyly.

"Hell yeah, Don, I'm tired of all this bullshit. You don't do anything to me and for me. Shit, I have to hold my own down and if that is the case, why the fuck I need you?”

“I’m not doing shit?” Don stated to Aunt Doll.

“Let those nasty ass motherfuckers help me take care of you. I can’t do it anymore!” Aunt Doll threatened. He picked up his clothes and before he could walk off, she said, “So, you really going to leave?”

He did not look at her. He smiled at us, and said, “Hell yeah, you told me to step, so I’m stepping. I’m a grown ass man and I run shit, but you want to play like this, fine with me.”

Aunt Doll ran to Don. She pulled and grabbed at him from the back. He never once faced her. Aunt Doll said as she cried like a baby, “Don, don’t go. I was wrong. You know I didn’t mean it. I was just talking. I didn’t realize what I was doing. You know I’m drunk and high on that shit. Wait until tomorrow so we can talk about it. Let me clear my head.”

He pretended to walk but slowed his pace as Aunt Doll held onto him tighter. Don stopped moving. “You need to stop smoking that shit because you be tripping. Once I move my shit back in, I’ll be damned if you throw my shit out again. I’ll leave this bitch and never come back. I can get another place to stay and better pussy at that. You better get your motherfucking mind right, Doll, throwing my shit out when I just had it pressed. Now you need to find a dick to suck so you can get my shit back right.”

“I will, Don. I promise, I will,” Aunt Doll pleaded.

He continued to look at us. Don turned around and pulled Aunt Doll close to him as he kissed her and fondled her ass. As Don groped Aunt Doll, he acted like he was all in love. A dude from my school drove by and blew his horn. Party turned around and waved at the nigga. I just kept staring at those two clowns, Aunt Doll and Don all hugged up. Bullshit. As Don and I met eye to eye, he looked at me and winked before Party turned back around.

He always tried to smile or blow kisses when he thought no one was looking. That was how snakes are; sneaky. You couldn't help but want Don. He was tall, with a dark brown, muscular frame, and clean cut faded hair style to match his smooth face. And, must I add, he was fine as hell to be a little over eighteen years older than us.

Bringing my thoughts back was the flash those beautiful, white teeth of his. He walked Aunt Doll back toward the car porch, and he got in the truck. He closed the door, turned the ignition on, backed up, and drove off toward the driveway. Once he got to where Party and I were, he winked at me and left. We stood and watched him drive on up the road. We both knew that he was going to the Gutta Sluts' house, but if Aunt Doll didn't care, why should we?

Chapter 2

"Why you let that motherfucker do you like that? He ain't worth more than a piece of shit in a toilet," Party spoke seriously.

"Bitch, you have never been in love. All you do is break up homes and not realize the whore shit you do around here," Aunt Doll replied with a little attitude.

"I know your ass can't talk. You know where he is and what he is doing, do something about it. Don't roll over and let his trick ass keep wiping his feet on you. He treats you like you don't even exist," Party said.

"Bitch, I'm going to leave your ass alone because I don't have time to make a damn bill that I don't intend to pay," Aunt Doll uttered to Party.

"I won't hit your bitch ass because you're my aunt, but you get out of line I will knock you the fuck out. If you play pussy today, you will get fucked today and if you play tomorrow, you will get fucked tomorrow" Party said as she looked at out aunt dead in her eyes.

"Hog, get ya damn girl before some shit jump off. If this bitch doesn't think her Aunt Doll won't whip ass, she will learn today, so keep yo ass in school," Aunt Doll said as she sat down under the car porch and lit her cigarette.

As Aunt Doll and Party continued to go back and forth

talking noise, I thought about Don. That big dick was always on my mind. My thoughts went back to when he first fucked me at age fifteen. At the time I thought his dick was so huge that he was gonna rip my pussy to pieces. I would never forget that day. Don came to pick up Party and me at a house party in Steeletown.

We were so drunk and high that night. We had smoked blunts, taking shotguns to the head, popping pills, and everything else with those niggas, plus, drinking all that Hennessy. Don dropped Party off at home first because he said he had to do the fatherly thing. I wasn't ready to get out, so we drove around. He took me to this little ass one hour hotel and fucked. I remember him pulling off my clothes and he...

"Hello, Earth to Mahogany," Party yelled out.

"What?"

"Damn, girl, what piece of dick got you in dream land?" she remarked.

"It's nothing, just thinking." I smiled as Aunt Doll handed me a beer and I handed it to Party. Aunt Doll then handed me mine.

"You must be thinking hard about that dick," Aunt Doll joked as she drank a swallow of beer.

"Why does it have to be a man? Just because you and Party are riding on niggas' dicks doesn't mean I'm thinking about one all the time," I added.

"Hog, you need to stop your damn lying. I know what you're thinking about, and that's fucking somebody's man," Party said.

I looked at Party, and then to Aunt Doll. A smile as big as a clown's spread across my face as I thought, *these bitches know me too well*.

"That's just like I thought," Party spoke as she drank her beer.

For a few moments, we sat under the car porch looking at cars go up and down the road. Aunt Doll gave me a cigarette to give to Party, and she lit herself another one. After a few puffs of her Seneca cigarette, Aunt Doll said as she laughed, "Don and I have the understanding that you trick off, you bring the money back home. It don't matter what dumb fucker you get it from." She looked at me, and sarcastically said, "He could bring me your money, Hog, and I will spend the hell out that shit."

"Aunt Doll, you don't have to worry about that because when he brings me your money, I spend the hell out that shit, too. Bitch, I don't care, either, it's just money and dick. Bitches need both to make it in this damn hood," I said.

Aunt Doll didn't reply right then because she was puffing on her cigarette with another can of Bud Light in her hand. Finally, she replied with slurred words, "Y'all bitches ain't game bread like me and my sisters. Other than the Gutta Sluts, we run this motherfucking hood. We have tricked off some of the motherfuckers you won't believe get down."

"What the fuck ever. We, at least I know, I can run circles around y'all old, tired ass whores and y'all still won't catch the clue. The men here are in need of young, hot, and, may I add, fresh pussy, not that shit they been getting for years," I spoke as I turned and gave Party a high-five.

"Here, pass Party one these beers," Aunt Doll said as she handed me the blunt, she had replaced for the cigarette. I inhaled deeply. That shit was fi! I took another long drag of the blunt and inhaled as long as I could. With my eyes closed, I felt relaxed as the smoke eased out my mouth in small circles. Before I handed it back to Aunt Doll, I gave Party a shotgun blow to the head.

As we sat under the car porch, an ambulance rushed by with about three police cars following. We all jumped up like criminals, but the 5-0 and ambulance left out as quickly as they came. We all looked at each other, ignored the shit, and continued smoking and drinking.

"You have to know what kind of dog you have. If you have one that barks, beware, he will soon bite. As for my dog, he is a beast and that is why I love that motherfucker so. He is not short stopping anywhere, y'all bitches hear me? He can do it all and he knows he has to be pleasing to me, that's why I keep his dog ass around," Aunt Doll said as she drank another beer.

"Awe, bitch, quit thinking about dick," Party said as if she was reading my mind.

"You think about dick, too, Party. Don't act like it's all her," Aunt Doll responded.

"Yeah, girl, you have your share of thoughts about fucking, too. I'm high as hell and need to get some sleep. C'mon, let's walk back up the road. It's getting late," I said to Party.

"Wait, I'll walk with y'all," Aunt Doll said.

"Didn't Don tell you to stay your begging ass here?" Party asked while I laughed.

"Yeah, you right, y'all go on. I don't have time to fuss and fight anymore tonight. I need to fuck," Aunt Doll said as she put her cigarette out and went inside.

Party and I walked back up the road high as hell and hungry. When we got on top of Billy Goat Hill, we looked across the street, down the driveway and saw Don letting out who appeared to be Pinky. He didn't see us, but we didn't care if he did or not.

We said our goodbyes as Party went to the left in her white house and I went to the right to the red trimmed mobile home. I didn't go in. I stood in the yard and continued to look down the long driveway across the street from us because the ambulance and police cars were in their yard. Pinky yelled something about a baby dead.

I couldn't quite understand from all the yelling she was doing and did not want my high blown. I was about to go in but stopping in my tracks, I paused for a second. I thought I heard someone in the shed. Realizing the shed was quiet; I continued to walk on up the doorsteps drunk and high than a motherfucker.

I went to the fridge and ate a bowl of cereal because there was nothing else. Besides, I was not about to cook a damn thing. While putting the bowl in the sink, mama jumped out of nowhere, scaring the shit out of me, "Damn, Pan!" I yelled because I knew as soon as she opened her mouth, she would have blown my high.

"I didn't say anything, Mahogany!" she snapped back.

She never called me by my real name unless something was bothering her. Seeing that she was sitting in the living room, I looked back and gave Pan half a smile as I continued into my room. As soon as I locked my room door, I heard a car and saw Don out my window. That nigga really be spitting some real ass game on those bitches. I couldn't talk because I was caught in the trap too, "That good dick motherfucker," I spoke with envy.

A few minutes passed and I heard the ambulance and police cars out the driveway. Walking over to my mirror, I stared at myself; I admired my beautiful, caramel skin tone. For a hood chick, I was very pretty. I had niggas lined up to fuck me, but I only wanted one man and that was Don.

Closing my eyes, I could imagine him fondling my perky breasts, his hands all over my body violating me over and over like a mad man. Halting my thoughts was the sound of a second car passing. Walking over to the window, I closed my blinds, took off my clothes, and got into bed. I was going to wash my ass, but I would do it the morning.

Folding my arms behind my head, I looked up at the ceiling. I continued to think about Don and the night he came over. On that night, my mama was on one of her crack binges. He and I talked and got high. He must have known that when I got high, I was ready to have somebody fuck me. Without too much more conversation, we ended up in my room.

There, on my bed was I, ready and more than willing. Taking off his clothes, he became hesitant to get between my legs. However, my eyes were on his raised manhood as it hung swollen between his legs. From the sway of it, the dick was ready to take me to another level. That night, the big dick belonged to me. Yes, my pussy was dripping wet from wanting him.

I spread my legs, and he began rubbing my clit gently as I moaned from the sensation. Sighing from that memory, my hands went down below, and I began caressing my pussy, opening and inserting my fingers with every other rub. *Damn, this feels good.* The better it felt, the more I began moving as I remembered Don's massive dick.

There was no way I could stop what I felt. The fingers pleased me, and I needed it, especially after I drank. The closer I got to my orgasm, the quicker my fingers worked. Without further ado, I froze as I yelled out his name. After busting my nut, I looked over at my door only to see a shadow move away. *Damn, I hope mama didn't hear me.*

Chapter 3

"Where my bitch at? Get your sleepy ass up and come fuck with me."

I looked up and there stood my bitch, Isis, known as Ice. *I thought I locked the door, how the hell she got in?* Anyway, Ice was a distant cousin. People said we were kin, but I didn't see how. I couldn't link her to any of my peeps, but it didn't matter. I wiped eye boogers out my eyes and sat up in the bed. I couldn't believe she was there. She hadn't been around in a minute.

Since she worked at the Capitol building in Jackson, she vaguely came down. She was stacking her paper so she could leave for Las Vegas to work the strip. She was just like me and Party, but on a higher level. She didn't fuck around with dick in the hood because her dick came from bigger fish in the Capitol building. All her niggas were powerful, white, rich ass intelligent niggas that didn't deal with penny shit like the broke bastards in the hood were.

I looked up to her because she had it going on and if I get this school shit right, I'd get hooked up with bastards like that. She was dirty and sneaky at the same time. As long as she didn't fuck behind Party or me, we were cool. Another reason Ice was cool was because we could go out and didn't have to worry about buying shit. She always had the hook up on everything, mainly the beer, weed, and gin, three of our favorites.

"Where you been, trick? You left us and hadn't looked back in a few months now," I asked her joyfully.

"It's Labor Day and I don't have to go to work today, but tomorrow I have to get at that shit. Get yo' bitch ass up so we can get into some shit tonight. I got the hook up at the Arab store and I don't have long to get there before the manager get back, so hurry the fuck up if you riding with us," Ice said as she walked out my room door.

I got up and put on some clothes to go outside. When I opened the front door, Party and Ice were already in the car waiting on me. I grabbed my knife because I didn't ride anywhere without it. When I got in the car, Party spoke to Ice,

"Bitch, how long you chilling?"

"Depends on how fucked up I get," she replied with laughter.

"You know she is here for a freebie," I said.

Ice looked up in the rear-view mirror, and said, "Can't be too much of a freebie if I'm supplying the damn beer and shit today."

We laughed, and I replied, "That's one reason why I like fucking off with you. You know how to show a motherfucker a good time."

"That shit is for real. You our nigga," Party said.

We laughed more and Ice turned up the tunes to drown

my voice out, but that was cool because I was chilling with my best buds in the entire world. Ice pulled up at Chevron on Hwy 35. They went inside and Ice bought beer, ice, cigarillos, and some type of daiquiri pouches. My stomach growled, so I left them to pack the car, while I went across the street to McDonald's for some burgers and fries. I walked back out and they were outside waiting on me. I had to squeeze in her Jaguar because beer cases were everywhere.

"This bitch sitting low, what all the hell you get, Ice?" I asked with amusement.

"You know how she does it and what she gets," Party said as she laughed.

"I told you that I had the damn hook up, my nigga. We gonna get drunk and fuck up somebody world tonight," Ice replied.

"Wait, let me go get an apple pie," Party said as I finally squeezed in the car.

Party didn't walk but a few paces from the car when she saw her ex-boyfriend's new girl pull up. Ice rolled down the window to see what was up because her eyes were focused on Party. She looked serious than a motherfucker. Party walked a few more paces until she heard, "You stupid whore, why you sweating my man? He is not yours anymore."

When I saw the way Party looked, I knew that apple pies were not on her mind anymore. Before the girl could say anything else, Party hit her in the mouth. Ironically, she tried to open the car door to get out, but Party was already pulling her out by her hair. Those crazy ass females were fighting over dick. The passenger stayed in the car. Even though, I was stuffed in the car, I jumped out quickly with Ice to keep it a one on one.

Ice went to the passenger side door and stood there. Her job, as always, was to make sure no one else jumped us when we were kicking somebody ass. But that day I stood with Ice because Party was stomping that girl's ass in the cement. She didn't need my help. After a quick stomping of Party's feet, I felt sorry for the girl and went to get Party off her. Her short ass could be a handful. On a few occasions, she had hit me because I was trying to stop her from doing some damage to someone.

When I finally pulled Party off the girl, people were standing around trying to see what was going on. Party up was kicking in the air. She yelled, "Bring your ass and your click to Billy Goat Hill. I'm gonna stomp that ass again. Go clean yourself up, motherfucker, you bleeding!"

Soon as we jumped in the car, we saw the cops. Ice drove off quickly because she knew that she couldn't afford to lose her job by getting in trouble. On the way back, we talked about the fight and Ice was more excited than we were.

"I haven't had this kind of fun since I left the hood," Ice said, almost out of breath.

"If Hog hadn't pulled me off her, I would have put that girl in a coma. And, I didn't get those apple pies, either," Party said as she held her hand back for her food.

I gave them their cold food. I didn't know about them, but I had to eat before I drank. If I didn't, I would be sick as hell the next morning.

"If I get as drunk as I think I am, shit, you will be catching the bus alone tomorrow and to be honest, I plan to get fucked up. I'm not learning shit in that bitch, anyway. The streets are my life. It's here that I get what I want. I don't have to be told when to go piss or not," Party spoke harshly as she turned her eyes toward Isis.

"You crazy, fool. I can go to the bathroom when I want, I just can't do it doing during court session," Ice giggled.

We laughed because Party always talked real shit, and most of it was right. The streets showed us a lot and it was through them that we saw that it was either to be on your hustle, improve your grind, or be lost in the world we call society.

Arriving back at the house, Bone was firing up the grill and it smelled good. A few of Bone's and Rabbit's hood friends unloaded the car. I used to have my eye on the tall thug, but he wasn't that goon type nigga for me. He was nice, but he used to fuck Ice. I know she wanted him for the night but if I got to that dick first, oh well. The short one used to nag Party since she gave him a taste of her pussy, now he wouldn't leave her alone.

The rest of the guys there I didn't know but seen them before. They were always around with Party's brothers and always tried to fuck me. It didn't bother me because I knew

Party had fucked them all. I went in the house and two more guys were in there playing Madden. I excused myself and went to the kitchen. Suddenly, I heard a voice coming from the living room. The female voice sounded very familiar, but I couldn't see her because she was almost behind the front door entry. I began to listen to their conversation.

"Damn, baby, where you come from?" one of the men said, and the other one laughed. "You look like you need some dick in your life. Didn't you call our names?" he added.

"Give me twenty dollars, I need a hit."

"Shit, I give no bitch money, but I'll give her the shit she needs," he replied.

"What you want me to do and when?"

"We can quit playing this game and go somewhere right now and play another game. Shit, I need my dick sucked and I want to know if you have a bad mouthpiece," that nigga spoke.

"I need to get up in something," the other one replied while rubbing his dick through his pants.

"We can go to the shed, but money or crack first. I don't have time to fuck one of you slow motherfuckers up for skimming me out my package."

I didn't know the guy that was talking to her, but I knew it was my mama begging for a quick high as usual. Without listening anymore, I stuck my head through the living room curtain and there stood my mama, looking like a natural born crack head. She was not bad to look at, being only eighteen years older than me, and her outfit was banging. Mama had on a short shirt to show her belly ring, and her breasts were almost exposed. Her thong was seen above her booty shorts, and she reeked of drug fumes. Her long hair flowed along her shoulders and her lips were painted a juicy red.

"You're a stupid motherfucker. Sit your ass down and go somewhere else with that shit," I spoke harshly to her.

"Who you think you're talking to?" Mama yelled.

"You; your cheap, high ass. I hate to see your ass running around here begging niggas," I hissed at her.

"I'm cheap, but I guarantee that I get mine. Niggas run behind this sweet ass," Mama said as she rubbed her body sexually.

The men in the living room were quiet and checked Mama out as she put on a show for them. She deliberately wiggled her big breasts in front of them and bent over to drop it like it was hot. I laughed at her because her old ass had those dumb fuckers' attention. I left out to go get a beer and moments later, I saw Mama and the two men go behind Party's house. I knew she was going to the shed to fuck and give head. I didn't like seeing her like that, but shit; I wasn't going to give her my money so she could fuck it up. I could do that shit myself. She wouldn't be satisfied until she got that package or something, dumb bitch.

Forgetting about Mama, I started drinking. It began to

get late and everybody who was anybody was on Billy Goat Hill. Even the Gutta Sluts were there. Nobody tried to jump stupid, and I was having a damn good time. The music sounded good from the Plies CD, and the liquor began kicking in. I took two guns to the head, and I was feeling my buzz, but I knew it was not going to last long when I saw Aunt Doll standing a few feet away from Don.

"Don, bring your ass to me," Aunt Doll said as if she was the shit.

Don ignored her as he kept talking to Yogi. Everybody looked at Aunt Doll because she was making people stop having fun to see her show her ass.

"Don, didn't I tell you to bring your scheming ass to me, now!" Aunt Doll yelled, that time there was an echo.

Don continued the conversation with Yogi while Pinky licked her lips at him. He finished what he had to say them, and then he walked off to calm Aunt Doll down. She was beyond wasted and falling over on people as she waited for Don to come to her. She always came to our gatherings and acted a damn donkey. Sometimes, I wished she would stay at home because as close as she could be to Don, I couldn't even get him alone to taste him again.

"Why you talking to those bitches? They can't fuck you like me and they damn sure can't suck dick like me," Aunt Doll said to Don loudly as everyone looked on.

"You right, you can't fuck like us because your pussy is

sloppy and drunk tonight," Pinky replied why rubbing her sister's breasts.

"Doll, sit your sloppy drunk ass down and chill, I got this. Just shut the fuck up," Don snarled, getting pissed off.

"You want to waste your breath on those bitches?" Aunt Doll said as she fell on Don.

"Who you calling a bitch, bitch?" Yogi spoke, approaching her with attitude.

"You, you no good slut. Get your own motherfucking man and leave my piece of shit alone!" Aunt Doll yelled back.

"Motherfucker, you don't want this drama tonight. I'll give you a run for your money," Yogi spoke, almost up on Aunt Doll.

"Don, those bitches aren't giving you a place to stay, and they don't take care of you like I do. Again, why you talking to those Gutta Sluts? They ain't got shit worth having and will probably never have shit," Aunt Doll said as she wobbled.

"Don, take that drunken ass pussy bitch to the house and come back to some sober shit. We'll be waiting on that long, good ass dick," Yogi said as they walked even closer to Aunt Doll.

"Whoa, bitches. We cool and all, but Aunt Doll is family. You fuck with her on Billy Goat Hill, you gonna get fucked up," Party said as she balled up her fists.

"Party, this shit ain't got anything to do with you," Pinky replied, stepping to Party.

"Move out the way, everybody. I'm about to rip a motherfucking hole in this bitch ass. Like I said, you ain't about to fight my aunt," Party said. Everybody moved out the way in unison but Don. "There she go," Party said. She pointed at Aunt Doll, and added, "Hit that bitch. I got your back."

"How in the fuck are you going to tell Doll to hit me? That bitch ain't crazy, just like you ain't crazy!" Pinky blurted out with anger.

"Bitch, you don't want these problems. You know I'll stomp a mud hole off in your country ass," Party threatened as she was about to rush Pinky. I stuck out my arm to block her.

"Country? You fucking country, too, Party, don't act like you the shit," Pinky replied.

"I'm about to whip that ass," Party spoke as she tried to go around me.

Chill out, chill out, Party," Don spoke to his daughter.

He laughed, and rushing out from the back of the shed was Rabbit. He stood next to Party and jumped in. "Nobody is going to do a damn thing on the Hill." He turned to Aunt Doll, and said, "Sit the fuck down, Doll. You always get drunk and bring that shit up here. If you want to trip, take that shit down the road to your shit. We can't do a motherfucking thing without your jealous ass trying to ruin it. You love Don that much, put the motherfucker in your pocket so nobody else can play with him."

"I would; if I thought his big ass would fit," Aunt Doll said to mock Rabbit's smart remark.

"Why the fuck you talking to my auntie like that? Have you lost your damn mind? If she wants to check her nigga, let her check the motherfucker," Bone said, swerving when he talked.

"Bone, get your staggering ass out the way. Right now, you can't fight the gnats off your ass, so sit your drunk ass down before I lay your drunk ass down," Rabbit said as if he was an umpire making a safe sign. Everybody laughed.

"You ain't talking to me, I'm your big brother," Bone said in a slurred tone.

"Cut that shit out right damn now," Aunt Tee said as she spoke more, "Nobody going to do a fucking thing on Billy Goat Hill without me. Y'all motherfuckers chill the fuck out."

"Tell that motherfucker to go home," Aunt Doll said as she pointed at Don.

"He ain't got to go a motherfucking where. He's not tripping, you are. Take your drunk ass to the damn house," Aunt Tee replied.

"Bitch, you mad because I'm fucking him now," Aunt Doll slurred at Aunt Tee.

"Drunk bitch, Pan had him first, so how the hell you talking. You were the dumbest one of us to fall in love with that bullshit after we wiped our asses with him," Aunt Tee said as she got stirred.

"I'll walk her home," Ice announced.

"Damn, I'll help you," Uncle Willie said. He was our uncle, and that motherfucker was also my supposed to be my daddy. Both Pan and Uncle Willie were the best of the crack heads. I was told that Pan was stoned and out cold one day and Uncle Willie was caught fucking her. How in the fuck could a brother rape his sister? That was some fucked up shit, but it happened, and I was the proof. The music started playing. Uncle Willie got on the other side to help Ice take Aunt Doll to their house while Don started dancing with Pinky.

I got angry seeing Don with that bitch myself. After thirty minutes passed, I didn't see Ice come back up the road. I looked around for Party and she was probably getting fucked somewhere, so I decided to walk down the road to walk back up to the gathering with Uncle Willie and Ice. When I arrived to the front door I was about to knock, but my instincts told me to look through the window. I saw Uncle Willie and Ice fucking with the lights on, stupid ass fools.

Those two blew my fucking high. Uncle Willie, my daddy, my uncle, was screwing Ice, and she appeared to be enjoying it. I was stunned because I never saw that coming. I was sure they figured no one would come to disturb them because of the party on Billy Goat Hill. I stood there and watched my dad fuck the shit out of my girl.

He was long and put it in every hole imaginable. She gripped the couch when he put it in her ass. She was a warrior, and I gave her props for that. But I still couldn't believe that they were fucking like dogs. I wondered where the hell Aunt Doll was while they fucked. Right before he was about to explode, I hit the door. They scrammed for their clothes.

I yelled out loud, "Ice, you in there?"

She didn't say a word, but Uncle Willie came to the door, breathing hard and said, "What the hell you want? You haven't been coming down here wanting shit. You need to take your dumb ass back up the road. You didn't lose a damn thing in this house. Burn it."

"Oops, I spoiled you from getting your nut?" I teasingly said as I stepped off the porch and walked back up the road.

When I got on the hill, I got in rotation for the blunt. I hit it and closed my eyes, all I could see was Uncle Willie's thigh pushing inside of Ice. Quickly, I had to open my eyes, and I shook my head. Everyone looked at me, but I got some beer and tried to drink away the sight in my head. I sat on the small grass bank in front of my house with a six pack of Bud Light.

Ten minutes later, I saw Ice walking up the road. I stood back and checked her dog ass out. She pretended like she was drunk, but I knew the damn truth. She always sobered up after a good fucking. I acted like I didn't see her.

"Hog, what's up?"

"My dad standing up in your ass," I replied.

I clearly took her by surprise. She stood there stunned for a moment before saying, "It wasn't like that."

"Bitch, please. You don't have to explain to me. That is your fucking business. If you let his nasty ass fuck you for free, let him fuck you for free because he broke, anyway," I said.

"Don't be like that. I was drunk and you know how horny I get when I am drunk. He just happened to be there, and I didn't care who he was or if he had money," Ice said.

"You still my bitch," I said to Ice with a smile.

We hugged and I went towards the house to find Party coming out the shed.

"Bitch, who you back there fucking?" I spoke.

"That short, fat bastard," Party replied.

"Why you give him some more? You know he's really going to bug you now," I said as I gave Party a beer.

"I told him if he bugs me, he won't be able to hit this ass again, and he quickly agreed." She laughed.

I replied, "What about the money?"

"Whore, I know you didn't think that I laid down for the free?" Party replied.

"Bitch, you didn't say anything about it, so how was I to know?" I replied.

"Look at this. His dumb ass just got paid and he let me trick him out of three bing bings," she said as she put the money in her sock.

"Damn, his slow-moving ass paid you three hundred for what?" I asked.

"I let him suck and squeeze the breasts for a hundred, for another hundred I sucked his dick and let him cum on my face, and for the last hundred I was going to let him get in the pussy, so he laid on top of me but it wouldn't get it up because I had let him nut on my face. So, that was free," Party said as she knew she got him good.

"Where you about to go?" I asked Party.

"Get on this drank. Why, what's up?"

"Shit, about to dance," I replied.

I went to the dance floor and Don came up to me, and said, "Let me get that slow dance, shorty."

"Yeah," I replied.

It was dark and people were everywhere, so we walked to the middle of the yard where no one would pay any attention to us.

"You know I need some of that fire head you give. I

hadn't had it in a few years," Don said as he held me close, grinding on me.

I was feeling that shit. I was fucked up and ready to get fucked. He didn't make it any better by getting me hot. He remembered what I liked and was using it to his advantage. "So, you want the head I can give, huh?" I spoke.

"Not just the head, but the ass is good, too. It's a plus," Don said.

"What makes you think I will let you get it again? You're fucking my aunt now and whoever else. I hate for a bitch to jump retarded on me and I have to fuck her life up," I told him.

"Because you know my dick is good and, many times, I had you craving me. I know you'll run after it now," he said.

He was right. When I first started fucking, he was the one to break my virginity and every other day we were fucking like animals gone wild. No one suspected me fucking him, but shit, at that time I didn't care. We would even fuck in my Aunt Doll's bed. He would take it anywhere. I loved that wild shit we did, but I fell in love, and he couldn't leave her or any of the other women for me. I weaned off him until the other day when he winked at me. He opened up something and he knew it.

"I don't know about all that. That shit you talking about was then, this is now. I'm almost nineteen and not the water headed fifteen-year-old girl anymore," I said.

"I feel ya on that, but remember, I taught you what you know and then some. So, you saying I can't get that pussy again? The pussy I broke in and kept tuned up until it fell in love," he said.

"I'm not saying anything," I said.

"Jump up on me and let me hold you like I used to," he dared me.

I jumped up on with my skirt pushed up. He pushed my thong to the side and with no warning, he was inside me, making love to me in the air in front of all those people and no one paid any attention to us. They didn't give a fuck. The hood was wild and off the motherfucking chain. You saw a little bit of everything on Billy Goat Hill. However, it was quick and just as wild as I thought it would be.

When he came, he held me close, and whispered, "You better not give my pussy away. Come back to me, I need to start fucking you again, Mahogany."

I couldn't answer because he was the only one to ever call me by my real name. When the music was close to the end, I nutted and pulled him close to me. I cried out, "Whatever you want, this is yours. Don, this is yours."

He put me down. People walked off the floor and it appeared that nothing happened. I quickly pulled down my skirt. I got fucked in front of everyone and no one knew. He made me remember how good and exciting being with him could be. In my heart, I thought he had feelings for me and for the most I believed he did but that was then, I couldn't be the air-headed teenager anymore.

Chapter 4

"Guess what, Hog?" Party said when I came outside from doing my homework.

"What?" I asked because she seemed upset.

"Pinky says she is pregnant by Bone. We all know he can't have kids since that horse accident he had when he was ten," Party said.

"Well, what he say?" I asked.

"He said he was there, but he wasn't the only one," she replied.

"True, so why are you upset about it?" I asked.

"Because that whore claiming that she deserves the right to get money from all of us. That trick is mistaken. She can be with his child all she wants, but she better not ask me for shit," Party said.

"Let us go for a walk. That usually clears our head," I offered.

"No, you go on. I'm going to stay here in case that bitch comes trying to steal food from us or something," Party said.

"Well, I'm going to check on Aunt Doll before she goes fishing at Isaac Green Lake. Shit, I may go with her, I don't have shit else to do," I replied as I began to walk down the road.

When I got to Aunt Doll's house, she was gone but Don was still there. Soon as I saw him my pussy leaped for him, but I had to get her under control. I played it off by saying, "Where Aunt Doll?"

"She gone fishing and Uncle Willie is gone to One Way. You have the answers, so stop wasting time and let me gone and fuck you right," Don said.

Don walked in the house. I looked around and saw that our cousins were gone, and no one was around to see me go in the house. I went in and went straight for my Aunt Doll's bedroom. When I walked in, he was already naked and on hard. Being quick, I got on my knees and began tasting him. I remembered how he liked his balls squeezed as I went up and down on his stalk.

"Nobody could ever do that like you, Mahogany," Don said in a daze.

I went slower just for him to be mesmerized on me doing him and not those other trifling sluts. It didn't take long. He shot sweet tasting, long overdue nut all in my face, and I tried to drink him all. Don did not need to catch his breath. When he laid me on my back and began drilling me, I knew that nut was a practice nut.

He gave it to me like I had been bad. I hadn't experienced loving like that since he and I quit fucking around. In fact, there really hadn't been anyone but him because no one could do it like him. He put in much needed time on my ass for sho. The way he rough fucked me only made me cry out and want him more. I had always loved his fucking and that day he made me fall back in the pattern I had left almost four years ago.

When I reached my orgasm, he did not let me go. He kept on drilling me, driving me mad with pleasure. A bitch couldn't help but fall in love with Don's dick because it was made of gold and that day, I found out it was beyond platinum. Once he did turn me loose, I got on my knees in the bed. Facing his feet, I took the desired meat stick in my hand.

Seeing that it was oily from being inserted, my eyes glistened as I played with it. Realizing that time was at hand, I began to lick it up and down. "Ooh, good." Not only did I taste his juice, but delighting myself in mine. Don knew that I didn't mind shit like that, for I was his freak, a damn freak period.

Once Don got harder, he stood on the floor and hit it from the back, just the way I love it. He dog fucked me and made this pussy squirt on the bed sheet. The minute we were finished, we both laid there breathing heavily. I couldn't believe that I had been missing out on that piece of dick all because I wanted him to myself.

I thought about what Aunt Doll said under the car porch a little while back about a piece of a man. I liked having a piece of Don. Actually, I did not think I missed his piece of a loving, but I did. Breaking my thoughts, Don said, "I knew you had to bring that pussy on home to me. You haven't been fucking, have you? You skinned me up at first but once I got in, that pussy welcomed me back home" Don put on his shirt.

"No, I haven't been fucking since you. Maybe one or two niggas, but that has been it," I replied.

"Good, don't give that good shit away, but if you do make him pay big for it and bring me my damn cut. You hear me?" he said.

"Yeah, I hear you, but I don't trick off that much," I said as I used the towel, he gave me to wipe off.

"You need to start because how the hell else am I going to have money if you don't give it to me? This type of fucking doesn't come free," he said as he put on his clothes.

"You right, I'll start finding me a fool to trick off for the money. Since you're tripping," I said to please him as he walked behind me and up the hall.

I sat on the couch, and he stood in front of me. "Good, now come give me a little more head. I love the way your tongue ring tickles me."

Trying to pleasure him, I did as he asked, and I got heated again. I knew that Aunt Doll would be home and that did not faze me. Remembering how he liked it, I didn't waste any of his seed because if he didn't put it on my face that meant like a good girl, I was to swallow it all, even if I choked. When I sucked all the liquid from his dick I kissed the head, for I was done, and his legs were shaking.

"Head jobs like that can't be given out. That shit you do

make a nigga like me jump stupid. You hear me?" Don spoke as he tried walking around to shake off that final nut.
"Yeah, I hear you, but you can't be dicking down bitches, either," I spoke protectively.

He did not answer me. I went outside. About fifteen minutes later, Aunt Doll came back from fishing and frowned when she saw me sitting under the car porch.

"What is it?" I quickly asked her.

"What the fuck your whore ass doing here? You know damn well yo ass not allowed if I'm not here," Aunt Doll said.

"I came by to trick off with your dumb ass, but you were gone so I waited. Is that a problem?" I asked.

"It is if you sucking and fucking my dick," she said, trying to smell me.

"Bitch, get the fuck back. That dick is everybody's dick, and that dick has a lot of drama behind it." I laughed.

"You damn right it does because I brought that dick from nothing to something, and I'll be dammed if I let some younger pussy like you get in on his goods, you hear me, bitch?" Aunt Doll harshly spoke.

"Aunt Doll, from this point anybody can fuck your dick and if you accuse me, I just might fuck and suck yo dick," I said.

"Hey, hey, what is going on out here?" Don said as he

came outside.

"She's accusing me of sucking and fucking you," I stated.

He gave me that, "It's my pussy smile" as he spoke, "I haven't had the pussy but if you want, I'll take her now so you will know for sure I'm working her ass out overtime."

"Don, sit your ass down. It's bad enough that you've had all my sisters, and you fathered my niece, so leave Hog the fuck alone," she threatened.

"Chill the fuck out, Doll" he said as he walked over to me and started rubbing my breast.

"Get the fuck away from her. Hog; take yo no good ass up that damn road. You bitch, if I ever catch you sucking and fucking my dick, I'm going to whip your ass," Aunt Doll said.

"Aunt Doll, if that is the case, I promise, you better come with it," I said as I stepped off her porch and began walking toward the road.

When I got back up the road, I told Party all about Aunt Doll. She was ready to go to Aunt Doll's house and fuck her up, but I calmed her down. We sat under the tree in the yard and Party rolled one up. The first hit was music to my ears. I needed that, especially after being fucked like that because Don had my pussy throbbing for more. Moments later, Bone and Rabbit came to hang with us. Yogi brought some beer, and we all were chilling. The wind blew softly, and the mood was perfect.

Bone tried to holler at Pinky about the supposed to be baby, but she wouldn't hear it. After two cases of beer, four blunts, and five pints of gin straight, everybody felt good. Rabbit saw that Bone was about to ruin our high, so he took Bone's beer and drank it.

"You always drunk Bone. You never sober, and you always ask for a little swig of mine, but when I give it to you its gone. Later, you always claim that you didn't do it."

"Man, Rabbit, I ain't always drunk, but today is one of those days. You want to do it? Jump, nigga!" Bone said as he flinched at Rabbit.

In an instant, Rabbit jumped on Bone. They weren't fist fighting, only tussling and rolling around in the dirt. I politely got two cans of beer and sat on my porch to watch the dumb motherfuckers fight over nothing. Party tried to break it up, but she was too thrown off to do anything. Yogi tried to break it up, too, but that didn't go so well. Party went in the house and Yogi came over to sit beside me to watch them fight.

Once they realized that we were just watching, they broke it up and started talking about it. Aunt Tee walked out of the shed and got onto them. They each said the other one started it. She didn't believe them because they were drunk.

"Y'all need to go wash y'all stinking asses. Standing out here, y'all done got ripe as hell, ya stinking motherfuckers," Aunt Tee said as she walked back to her house. They still stood out there talking about it like it was a game, describing how each one did the other.

I looked at Yogi, and said, "Is your sister really pregnant by Bone?"

"Girl ain't no telling who that damn baby daddy is because she fucks like we fuck," she responded.

"Well, he ain't got no money, he ain't got no job, shit, and he still stays on Billy Goat Hill. She should have set her sights a little higher," I said as I drank more of my beer.

"He can't fuck because I done had him, too. But Don; shit, that motherfucker right there can eat some pussy and lick some ass. You hear me?" Yogi said with excitement.

I froze because Don had never ate me out and there, I was listening to this Gutta slut telling me that he ate her out and even licked her ass. I played it off and pretended not to let it bother me. I drank another swallow of my beer, and said, "I didn't know he eat pussy."

"That motherfucker can eat the hell out of some clit. Why you think every bitch here trying to give him the damn pussy? His ass has pussy lined up everywhere he goes. That bastard doesn't ever have to work 'cause bitches like us takes good care of him," she explained.

"Bitches like y'all take care of him? I don't have money to give no motherfucker. I'm barely living myself," I pointed out to her.

"I don't get it, Hog. I hear your ass smart as hell. Why

you still here? If it were me, I'll start my life over and not come back here for fear that I will fall back in the same predicament that I am in now," Yogi spoke as she lit her long ass Virginia Slim cigarette.

"That's a question I will answer when I graduate in May," I responded.

"Fuck this dumb shit here. I wouldn't have a baby or nothing. I love my child, but damn, it's hard out here and pussy doesn't sell like it used to. Too many motherfuckers practically giving it away," she joked with laughter.

"Hell yeah, my mama will put the average bitch to shame," I said as we laughed.

"Too much shit goes on here. It doesn't matter if it's Billy Goat Hill, Hunter Road, Steeletown, Jacktown, or Forest. Everybody fucking everybody, you can't have dick to yourself. And don't let it be good dick. You'll have to fight the bitch because she lost what you found," Yogi said with laughter as she spoke the truth.

"That is the damn truth. All this fucking the same dick gives The Hill, our hood, a bad name. Where are the good men at?" I asked as I laughed.

"Hog, you meet a good guy, right?" Yogi paused, waiting on me to agree. I bowed my head yes, and she said, "You meet a good guy, and you want to bring him to your family, but shit, you can't do that. You'll fuck up 'cause one of the motherfuckers gone tempt him to fuck them. From then on, it's everybody's dick."

"Bitch, you right. I don't think Party would do me like that," I said.

"She might not, but I don't put shit past a pair of lips hid out of sight, 'cause when pussy calls, it wants somebody to pick up the fucking phone because the bitch gone talk," Yogi spoke.

Party saw me and Yogi talking. She staggered over to us, and said, "What y'all whores talking about? Y'all bitches probably over here lying to each other."

"We talking about how bitches will trick off with your man. Shit, not just bitches, but your own family," I stated to see what she would say.

"Ain't nobody gonna fuck behind you, Hog. We have different taste, but you," Party said as she pointed at Yogi, "I've seen your men, they fine as hell. You have good taste in dick."

"You right about that, and the motherfuckers are going to spend that cake," Yogi said as she put her cigarette out and lit another one.

We heard some hollering and looked up and saw it was Pinky. She screamed out to Yogi in the middle of their long driveway, "Come get your damn baby, I can't sleep with him hollering and shit. You need to keep your ass at the fucking house, acting like you don't even have a child."

"Bitch, I'm coming. Can't you see I'm talking? Or are you blind? You need to get glasses or something," Yogi yelled back.

"I see y'all bitches later, I have to go get that damn boy of mine. His daddy needs to get him for the weekend, but the bastard is MIA," Yogi said as she cursed and walked off down to her driveway.

"Aight," I said behind her.

"Hog, I got to lay this ass down," Party spoke.

"Are you going to school tomorrow?" I asked.

"Hell no, thinking about quitting," Party said.

"Party, you can't learn at the house," I stated as she broke my high.

"Yes, the hell I can. I'm tired of getting up and for what? Listen to some boring ass teacher tell me about shit they ain't never been through. The streets teach me and take care of me," Party seriously spoke.

"Okay, I'm about to go lay this ass down, too. I'll get at you tomorrow when I get out," I said as I got up and went in the house.

When I walked in the house down the hall, I heard Mama say, "Will, whip your pussy."

I froze. She was in the room fucking her brother. What the fuck? I walked slowly to my room and stared at the ceiling. My thoughts began to race out of control. "It is bad enough that

I am a product of incest, but to know that my mom is still fucking her half-brother, it makes me sick. He was just fucking Ice the other night at the party. Now he is fucking my mama for what, a dub, a damn twenty-dollar bill?" I turned over to tune them out by hitting the wall because she was moaning like no one was in the house.

An hour passed. I woke up from dozing off and they were still fucking. I was getting annoyed about them going at it and carrying on. I got out my bed and before I could knock on her door, someone knocked on the front door. I went to the door and spoke loud enough for whoever was knocking to hear. "Who is it?"

"It's me, Don" the voice said.

Quickly, I opened the door and Don was standing there. I didn't let him in, but I spoke angrily, "What the fuck you want?"

"Whoa, shorty, why you being so mean?" he asked.

"I heard about you eating pussy, but not mine. What the fuck is up with that?" I replied, getting ready to slap the fuck out of him.

"Is this what your attitude is about?" he asked.

"Yes, I suck on you and your big ass balls all the time, but you won't return the favor," I said.

"Mahogany, I don't eat pussy or ass for that matter. Shit, if I do that, I guarantee she gave me money to do it," Don said.

"What about me and mine? You don't put your mouth on me, but you will put your mouth on some other whore," I said.

"Come on, baby girl, chill with that shit," he replied as he rubbed my face with the back of his hand.

"I just wanted to know, but don't worry about it. I won't let you get this pussy again," I continued, just to make him mad.

"You'll give me that pussy any damn time I want it," he spoke with assurance.

"Sure," I said as I walked off and went back to my room.

Moments later, Don walked in, and said, "Get on your back, I want some pussy."

"You think you do. I'm not those tricks you fuck around here," I replied.

"I know who I am fucking and right now, I choose to fuck you. Roll your ass over and give me my pussy," Don demanded.

I did as he asked because I wanted him, too. He was drunk and when he was on the gin, that dick stayed up. He would ride me all night before he came. That night, I didn't matter because I'd already had my period, and the pussy was all his. When he lifted my legs up and entered me, he was fierce. He was eager and quick in his thrusts. I had never had him take me so fast and brute before. He dug deep inside my pussy, and it was damn good. The best he had ever fucked me, to be honest.

Don was an animal. I threw it back to him and he caught every thrust I gave to him. I couldn't understand how demanding he was and how craved my body was for him. Our fucking was powerful as he was moaned and said my name in my ear. Psychologically, he was fucking with my head. He even said it was his pussy and all that good shit. I was crunk.

I loved for him to tell me things like that. He fucked me beyond my wildest dreams, and I delighted myself in him. Don stuck his big dick deeper than ever inside me and I swore I felt his balls enter me, too. But the most powerful part of the fucking was when he screamed in my ear that we were in love. Don made my body come alive and through all the sweat and musty smell of my small room, I truly felt that I had been made love to for the first time since he broke my virginity.

When we finished, he stared deep into my face, and said, "Your pussy makes me crazy, and I swear I have to keep coming back and getting some but tonight let me do this."

I didn't know what to expect, but when he put his tongue on me, I nearly leaped. My lover was doing what I heard Yogi said he did. He made me close my legs around him and tell him that I wouldn't fuck anyone but him. When he made me reach my peak, I was exhausted and worn out. I didn't even know when he left. I was sleeping like a baby. I was high on top of a high and I had Don to thank for the feeling I had received.

I woke up the next morning with a smile I had never had before. The man I had always loved told me that he loved me, too. I could not believe it and the saddest part was that I could not tell my best friend, my cousin, that not only was I fucking her dad, but I was still in love with him.

"Hog, come here," I heard Mama yell out.

I got out the bed, but my legs were wouldn't hold my weight. I yelled out, "One minute."

I finally stood up and took a few paces. I was sore, but a good sore. I needed that extra fucking he gave me. I put on my clothes and walked up the hall. Mama was sitting on the couch, and she was looking serious. I said, "I hadn't had time to bathe, so what is so urgent?"

"I think you should know that I love you with all my heart and if I could change who your father is I would, but according to the laws of physics I can't."

"You about to die or something? If you are, give me your money," I said to make a joke.

"No, I ain't going no damn where, but you might," she said.

"I might go where?" I asked.

"To the point of no return of your mess."

"Where is this point at, Pan?"

"The point is where you have lost your self-respect and your dignity. What reason for bettering yourself than to leave this damn Hill? Don't be like the rest of us," Mama said.

"Anyway, what you call me up here for?" I said as I was about to leave.

"You and Don fucking," Momma replied with disappointment on her face.

"Huh?" was all I could say because I didn't know what to think. "There's nothing to tell," I spoke.

"I know you are fucking him because Doll told Tee and Tee told me. What the fuck are you doing?" she said.

"I see," was all I could say.

"I know I am not the best role model for you to follow," she said.

I stopped her by saying, "No, you're not because I heard you screwing your own brother. Not only did you screw him, you had me as evidence."

"This is not about me and the horrible things I do. I am a drug addict and will eat your pussy if you have what I need. I have to draw the line. You can't keep fucking him. He means you no good. I've had him. In fact, I had him first. Your Aunt Tee had a child by him and your Aunt Doll loves him. I wish you would not fuck him again. What if he is really your dad and not Will? What do you think will happen to you and Party when she finds out about you fucking her dad?"

"First of all, I hadn't been fucking him," I denied.

"Hog, I am an old whore in the game, and I know better, so you can cut the crap with me. I know you fucking him and I know he loves you," she replied with concern for the first time since I don't know when.

"He loves me?" I questioned as my eyes lit up.

"No, silly, get your head out the damn clouds. He is only using you and you just confirmed what you tried to hide. Your face lit up when I said that. He only wants you as the young flavor this time, but what about the countless of other women he is fucking on a daily basis? Your Aunt Doll being one of them, and me from time to time," she said as she lit her cigarette.

"Well, Mama, I know what I am doing and to be honest with you, if I wanted him, I'll take him," I pointed out to her.

"Yeah, you and how many other dumb ass bitches have tried? He has been around the block more than you can imagine. Did you know he used to fuck his own daughter?" Mom said.

"Who, Party?" I asked.

"No, he has another daughter y'all age. He fucked her and got her pregnant. She had the baby, but she hates her own child because it is a reminder of what she did. I don't want you to fall for that type. It is bad enough that I fucked my half-brother for a little of nothing and had a child out of incest. Look, Hog, there are other nice guys out there. Just get out the hood and don't limit yourself as Party does. She only wants to fuck the hood, but you, my daughter, you are smart and can do better," Mama said.

"Really?" I said to patronize her.

"Hog, I am serious. If I didn't love you, I wouldn't be trying to warn you. Don is probably trying to fuck someone in our family now. It is bad enough that I fucked his cheap ass two or three days a week for the last four months, but to know that my daughter is getting the same dick I am getting. It has to stop. When I fucked Don, it wasn't worth it, but I needed the high. He has been the main one I have been fucking, because he supplies me with the best Caine this side of Mississippi. I tell you I can't help it but wish I could. I really don't want us to be fucking him, mainly you because you are young and because it is my sister's boyfriend and my other sister's child's father," Mama said as she opened a wine cooler.

"You had him last week and weeks before that?" I asked.

"Yeah, right here on the couch. He was impatient and I was ready to get high. He had the ten I needed, and I gave him a few minutes of my time. It didn't last long, and I don't regret it. Not until I can get off these drugs because I do things I never thought I would do. I don't want you to end up like me and in love with a thug ass nigga that means you no good. I may be an addict, but I can tell you every time a man digs in my ass. If I get anything, I will know the source," she said as she swallowed her wine cooler.

"If you meet a nice guy, you can't bring him to this family because all y'all trick ass bitches would try to fuck him for his cash or whatever. So, I would rather leave the nice guys to the nice bitches and be a hustler like you," I said.

"Fine, you hardheaded ass bitch. I tried to warn you, so don't come asking me for advice when he knocks you up and you look like boo boo the fool," she replied with a little anger.

Chapter 5

I went to the bathroom and while I was in the shower, my mind lingered on what Mama had said. The worse part about it was I believed every word she said. I was being selfish and inconsiderate of what this could do to my relationship with Party. We swore not to fuck behind the other, but we never said anything about dads. I stayed in the shower longer because I knew that I have to tell her before any of my bitch ass aunts told her something totally different.

Putting on my clothes, I went out the door to Party's house, but she went to school. *Isn't this shit? I didn't go, but she took her drunk ass on*, I thought as I smiled. *At least I have a few hours before she got home to work on my speech.*

I had nowhere to go and nothing to do. I decided to check out the college brochures and start applying. I had never thrown myself into anything before until then. I was really considering leaving Billy Goat Hill because I took inventory. The Gutta Slut was right. We all were fucking in circles and if one got something, it would be hard to pinpoint where the source was.

Deciding to get out the house, I walked outside. I didn't see anyone stirring, so I decided to go see what Aunt Tee had cooked. I walked over to her house and slipped in. Walking into the house, I heard the familiar words, "This is my pussy. It belongs to me. I love you." I felt sick, but I had to go see.

I know fucking well that Don wasn't in that bitch fucking my Aunt Tee, too. I opened the door and there in my vision was the man that just told me that he loved me and now he was fucking my other aunt. He was so engrossed in sexing her that he didn't know I was standing there, or if he did, he didn't care. I stayed there unable to move, watching the entire scene.

He made her feel the same way he had me as he grinds her forcefully. I didn't know what to think and I didn't know what to do. No matter what I tried, I couldn't remove my eyes from the sight in the bed. Aunt Tee made him scream out loud, something I had never done to him. A tear fell from my eye. I was heartbroken all over again and disgusted.

When he finished, Aunt Tee said, "Get your ass out my room, can't you see I was fucking?"

Don turned over and looked at me. He didn't say a word, he kept touching Aunt Tee's breast. Quietly, I closed the door and ran to the bathroom. I vomited all over the seat and floor. I was sick to my stomach. I wiped my mouth and got up off the floor. I went outside to the tree and sat there. I felt like the damn fool I was. There I was giving myself to a man that gave his self too many women freely. It was then that I realized I couldn't casually fuck because I got attached. I sighed and I remembered that I hadn't eaten yet, but I wasn't hungry. I saw the bus.

Party got off the bus, and said, "You missed the damn bus. When I saw that you were not going, I wanted to run back, but shit, it was too late. I was already up and dressed. What's up with you?"

"We need to talk," I said.

She threw her books on the stool outside, and said, "Where the beer?"

"We out," I stated.

"Okay, what we need to talk about?" Party said.

"Well, to be honest, I had fucked your daddy and thought I was in love with him. We had been fucking for a long time, and then I stopped. We started back the other night and I'm so sorry," I said plainly.

She looked at me, and said, "Bitch, are you dumb? He only loves himself and for you to fall weak to the game is bullshit. I thought I taught you better than that. Bitch, I thought you were smart?"

"I did fall prey to his cunning ways and deceitful manner. I was tricked and today, I caught him with your mom," I said.

"Bitch, if you told me I would have told you that they still been fucking and Aunt Doll knows it, too, but with you that is deep. That's a hard ass pill to swallow," Party said.

"I'm so sorry. We still girls?" I asked her.

"Hell yeah. We didn't include not fucking the other's dad, only niggas we love. So yeah, you still my number one bitch," Party said as she got up to go change clothes.

I didn't know what else to say. I told my girl the truth and she was rather calm about the situation, but if I knew her like I did, I knew she was going to fuck someone I loved, and at that moment I was in love with her father. I was thankful that I had no guy in general that I wanted for if I did, Party would fuck my world up because I believed that I hurt her today. Damn.

Moments later, Party walked out of the house with her regular clothes on. We walked toward the Gutta Sluts' driveway. Deciding to go to the end of our road, we made it to Old Jackson. Usually, we turned around but today we went to Oliver Drive and sat by the big pond, hoping to get a glimpse of the alligator that we used to hear about.

We started throwing pebbles into the water and reminisced about when we were younger and the games we used to play. I didn't think she remembered all the memories, but she did. Some of the memories I was sketchy about, but she told me how it went, and she was right. Everything was wonderful as my best friend, and I sat along the pond bank and shared memories.

"What made you sleep with my daddy? I mean, I expected better from you," Party asked out the blue as she threw pebbles into the pond.

Deciding to tell her about the first time and not the recent time because it is suspect; therefore, I will say it is the only time. Clearing my voice I spoke, "You and I had got drunk in Steeletown. Don let you out and I did not want to get out. He came on to me and I did it. He was my first time, and I thought it was special."

"You didn't have to fuck him. Didn't you know he was fucking the rest of them?" Party said as she never looked my way.

"I did, but I couldn't explain the yearning between my legs. He told me it was natural to want him because the rest of them wanted him and if it were wrong, then why are they all still sleeping with him? To a fifteen-year-old, it made sense, and I didn't look at it in another way," I said.

I realized at moment that she was going to do something to hurt me because I fallen victim to her daddy's trap like the rest of the hood. I understood her pain because our parents were no good. I smirked because she was not the daughter of incest and her mom was screwing everybody, but mine was screwing for nickels and dimes. *Isn't that a bitch?* I thought as I said, "Party, I will not ever sleep with your daddy again and I have not slept with anyone that you ever had or wanted."

"I know, but the best thing about it is you still my girl and at least you didn't get knocked up by him."

"Come on, I know somebody has some beer, gin, or something for us to drink. A bitch is thirsty," I said as we got up and started walking.

We made it back to Billy Goat Hill. Aunt Doll and Aunt

Tee were in the yard arguing. Mama sat on her steps looking, probably because she was too stoned to move or do anything about it. Party ran up on Aunt Doll, and said, "What the fuck is the problem here?"

"That trick ass momma of yours gave Don a disease," Aunt Doll said.

"How the hell is that when I just screwed him today? Ask Hog, she caught us," Aunt Tee said.

They all turned to look at me. I said, "What the fuck y'all staring at? I wasn't fucking him."

"Awe, bitch, don't go there," Aunt Doll said.

"Don't' go where?" I asked.

"You fucked him on the dance floor at the party. Your face looks fat, ya ass might be pregnant and if you are, I'm going to cut it out of you," Aunt Doll said.

"Shut the fuck up. I'm not pregnant and I didn't screw him on any dance floor," I lied as I walked up on her.

"Yo bitch ass might have given him the damn disease because he doesn't go too many places without you," Aunt Tee said.

Aunt Doll turned her head toward Aunt Tee and Party. I stood there because with her mentioning a disease, that threw a new ball in the game. I did have sex with him and no protection was ever used. Before I knew it, Aunt Doll swung on Party and

Aunt Tee. They were all rolling on the ground and I decided to get in to get me a few licks off that big, mouthed ass Aunt Doll. We were all going back and forth, pulling hair and biting each other.

I just swung and hoped that I hit Aunt Tee as well for screwing Don. Party yanked and pulled on Aunt Doll's hair as I started to pull them a part. I knew that being in love was dangerous, but to front on every woman that had ever had him was explosive. Aunt Doll didn't care. She loved Don with all her heart, and she didn't care if everybody slept with him as long as he came back to her. I could feel her torture of loving a no good man because I loved him, too.

I finally broke up the fight and Aunt Doll went back down the road to her house to fight with Don. Uncle Willie came out our house and walked over to where we all stood. "He is fucking anything with a pussy. All y'all bitches need to sit the fuck down arguing over neighborhood dick. Y'all some silly bitches, if I ever did know any in my life, fighting over dick none of you will have to yourself is stupid." Uncle Willie looked over at me, and I pretended not to see him. He went on to say, "Doll too damn stupid to see that he isn't worth the air he breathes."

"I wouldn't say that. He is still my daddy no matter how fucked up this shit is," Party said as she looked at Uncle Willie.

"Yeah, he did create a good-looking thing like you. Come here, Party, I want to have some fun," Uncle Willie said with a tease.

"Sit your nasty ass down," I said because the look on Party's face was priceless.

After a long day, it was almost nine p.m. I decided to pretend to be sleepy and went home, for a lot was on my mind. I peeped out the window and Aunt Tee had gone. Mama was on the couch asleep, and then I saw Party and Uncle Willie go to the shed. My heart sank because I knew she was only going to do it because she found out I had fucked her daddy. The best of me had to see, so I eased out the back door. Stepping on the five-gallon bucket, I got lucky because the light from the moon displayed their body prints through the window.

There, on the mattress, was my girl. She was giving my dad head. I wanted to gag because not only was she acting like a pro, but she was all slutty with it. He cupped the back of her head with his hand and banged her face between his legs. He was fucking Party in the mouth. She was enjoying it because I remembered how she said she acted when she enjoyed what she did. I eased off the bucket and dropped my head. *I could disturb them, but for what?* I thought as I went to my house. *Let her do what she does because I did it to her first. Maybe we will be even.*

As I climbed into bed, my mind went back to how I thought I knew how she felt, but now I knew for sure how she felt. It didn't feel right. It was something about fucking a friend's daddy and even if they were kin, it still placed agony in my chest. I pulled the covers over me and curled up because something was not agreeing with me.

As I tried to sleep, my mind went back to Aunt Doll's words, she might be pregnant, and she might have given Don that STD. I tossed and turned thinking about that shit all night. Damn, was it too late?

Everything cooled down and before we knew it, November had arrived, and Party decided to start her Thanksgiving holiday three weeks early. Lucky for me, every chance I got her dad was digging deep in my pussy. Nevertheless, all morning I couldn't eat. I didn't know what to think. The stomach virus had been going around because three days earlier, Rabbit had it and I felt like I had it. The difference was I wasn't running off, I was constipated and felt like throwing up.

All during school I kept my head down. I didn't feel much like answering questions in class and I sure as hell didn't want anything to eat. My teacher saw that I was sick and gave me a hall pass to go see the nurse. I wasn't going to go but figured why not because I needed to feel better for the upcoming party on Thursday. I walked into the office, signed in, and she directed me to have a seat on the padded table.

"Ms. Mahogany Jeffers, what seems to be bothering you on this last day?" The nurse asked as she waited for me to answer.

"I think I have some type of virus because I am constipated and sick on the stomach. My appetite has changed. I'm eating more and more, but sometimes it wants to come up but doesn't," I said as I waited for her to say something.

She got up and went to the cabinet. She came back with a small white cup in her hand. She said, "Go and urinate in this cup. When you are finished, bring the cup back to me."

I took the cup from her and did as she said. She went to the other side of the office with my piss. Moments later, she came back, sat down, and said, "Ms. Jeffers, I understand that you are an honor student in spite of the bad girl image you try to portray, but you should know that you don't have a virus."

"Okay, then give me my medicine so I can feel better," I said.

She smiled as she said, "Ms. Jeffers, you pregnant. Congratulations."

"What the fuck did you say?" I spoke offensively.

"Control your tongue. I said you are pregnant," the nurse repeated.

"How could this have happened? Even if I don't remember him putting on a damn condom," I spoke out loud angrily.

"Ms. Jeffers, I assure you that having sex is how a baby happened," the nurse spoke as she wrote me a prescription.

"What are you doing?" I asked her with tears in my eyes.

"You need your vitamins so the baby can be healthy," she said.

"You can keep those damn vitamins. I don't believe I'm keeping it. I don't want any fucking baby," I said as tears flowed.

"Ms. Jeffers, this is a big decision. Right now, your hormones are racing, and you are not thinking clearly. Talk to your parents, talk to the father. Do you know who the father is or is there some other type of situation that makes you not want the child?" she said.

"Bitch, do you know who your father is?" I said as I laid my head down and cried.

"I understand that you are upset but calling me a vile name is not the problem. You must decide on what to do although the baby is a living being. You don't want to kill a living soul, do you?" the nurse said as she placed her arm around me to comfort me.

"I'm not dumb, but since you really want to know why I don't want it let me tell you this. My mother and aunts all share the same man. He is the father of my best friend and the father of my child," I said to watch her mouth drop open. "To top it off, my mother slept with her brother and here I am. Everybody on Billy Goat Hill is fucked up in some way or the other."

I got up and walked to the door. I turned to her, and said, "Now you see why I don't want the baby. This pregnancy is just going to add more fire to the fuel. All those bitches are going to hate me, including my best friend."

I closed the door and walked to the bus, for the bell just

rang for us to go home. Getting on the bus was hard. I knew that I would see my girl, but the hard part was not telling her or anyone on The Hill for that matter. When the bus door opened, I didn't see her. I felt relieved. I stood in the driveway and walked toward my mobile home on the right. Aunt Tee came to the door, and said, "Why you looking so gloom, Hog? You look like you lost your best friend."

"Had a long, boring day and it doesn't appear to get any better," was my reply.

"Well, today is Tuesday. You'll cheer up when Party get back on Thanksgiving Day," Aunt Tee said.

"I thought she was just not going to go to school. I had no idea that she actually left. Where she go to, anyway?" I asked.

"She's gone to Ice's crib. She said to tell you to try and get Bone or Rabbit to bring you because Ice's car is in the shop. An old, white woman hit her from the back when she was pulling onto State Street over in Jackson," Aunt Tee said.

"Damn, she didn't get hurt, did she?" I questioned.

"Naw, she okay, but was a little shook up, I think," Aunt Tee said.

"That's good. You see Mama today?" I asked.

"I saw Pan earlier, but that was when she came out the shed and left with somebody from Steeletown in a maroon truck, I think."

"Okay. I might ride down there where my girl at later. If I get a ride, but doubt it," I said as I walked toward my mobile home on the right.

Once I closed the door, I locked it. I didn't want to be disturbed because mama was gone probably for the next night or two. Who knows, she always tricked off for days at a time and practically allowed me to raise my damn self. *Some fucking loving home I come out of,* I thought as I ran to the bathroom to vomit.

When I finished, I changed into my night clothes because I wasn't going out the door and I wasn't expecting company. If anyone came, they were not getting in. I went to my room and got in the bed. I got on my back and the thoughts kept coming. *Do you think Party would forgive you? What do you think Aunt Doll would say or what would Don say? Do you think he would accept the baby? Do you think he would really show you love because you carrying his child? How about taking care of it? You don't trick off enough to make serious money to support a child and a drug addicted mother. Could you look at the child and not hate it as his other child does with her child? What are you going to do? How are you going to do it?*

I jumped up and placed my hands to my ears. I screamed out loud to my conscious, "Shut the hell up!" My thoughts became void as I began to sob uncontrollably. I was smart but made a dumb decision. It never really occurred to me about getting off the Hill. That was something no one here planned to do. I loved my girl Party, but I got caught up with a baby. I would have assumed that she would get caught up before me, but that was not the case.

Closing my eyes I tried to sleep, but sleep would not come. I tossed and turned for hours and still no sleep. I got up, sat on the back porch, and lit a blunt I had hid for emergencies. When I got halfway finished, I saw Mama walking out the shed. She stood a few feet from it to look like she was just standing there. Quickly, I put the blunt out and waited to see if she saw me, but she didn't. Seconds later, I wanted to scream. Don walked out behind her, put his arms around her, and held her like he had done me. I couldn't remove my eyes from them, so I watched and listened.

"Pan, what the fuck was I thinking to fuck off with those other bitches? Your pussy is the best and you give fire ass head," Don said as he held Mama from the back and kissed the top of her head.

"Don, we have been through so much together. Long before you met my sisters, you know. You should be mine in public and not behind closed doors all the time," she said as she appeared to snuggle closer to him.

"Baby, I have been through more with you than anyone alive. Shit, you were there for me when we were in junior high. Shit, we have always been together, and no one can stop me from loving you the way I do. Pan, you will always have my heart, no matter what hand life deals us. You have been there for me before I became who I am. But shit, life happened, and I got surrounded by the streets, whores and the survival. You couldn't hack my new lifestyle, and we had to call it truce, but now it's different, you feel me? If I had to start over again, it'll be you and only you. No Doll, Tee, or any of the other dumb bitches I'm fucking," Don said.

"I know. I feel the same way, but shit, too much has happened, and we can't pretend that you haven't fucked everything in the hood from Billy Goat Hill to wherever for that matter," she replied with a vague smile.

I wanted to die and go to Hell right there. For some reason, I believed what he told Mama. I had never heard him speak the way he had that night. I had no reason not to believe him. I knew Mama said she knew him, but I had no idea that she went that far back with him. It never occurred to me that they had that much history. I just assumed that Don had always been a whore.

"Don, you know Hog fancies you and I know that you fucked her that night you came to get Uncle Willie. I was pissed off so bad that I couldn't enjoy my nut, especially after I heard her enjoying that dick, that slutty daughter of mine. I almost stop fucking to whip her ass, but shit, I had a job to do," she spoke with passion in her words.

"Shit, I don't want her. She's my daughter's age. I only did it to get back at you because she wasn't my child by you. Instead, you had her by that slow ass, big mouth Willie. I can't stand his nosy ass sometimes because he'll help me do shit, and then run his damn mouth. I'm just glad she looks just like you. Maybe you should look at those results again," Don said.

"Don, that was a little over nineteen years ago and you still hold that over my head? I was on drugs," she replied as she tilted her head to the sound of Don's breathing.

"Hell yeah," Don spoke loudly. Mama laughed. "Shit, I got to get a baby in yo ass so I can have a reason to fuck you all the time instead of all this creeping and shit. I don't like the fact that any and every dick goes in and out the pussy and mouth I love," Don said.

"Well, I had Willie that night, but other than that I haven't had anyone but you in a while now. I have sucked dick and ate pussy lately, can't lie, but it has always been your dick I came back for," she replied while staring at him.

With tears flowing everywhere, it got hard to muffle my cry. I couldn't open the back door because the small light would show, so I threw a bottle toward them in the woods. They scurried away. Don cut through our front yard and went back down the road while Mama went inside Aunt Tee's house.

Bone came outside and went behind their house to tie up the screen door. He saw me and came over. "Why yo ass sitting in the dark? Your ass up to something?" he asked.

"No, just listening to the night. You know it has ears?" I said, trying to hide my tone.

"What's wrong with you?" Bone asked.

"Shit, just tired, plus, my partner in crime gone," I replied.

"Hog, I know tired when I see it and you are not just tired," he said as he lifted his hand to wipe away my tears. "Who has made you cry? I'll fuck that bitch up. Show me where he's at and I'll get him," Bone said as he looked around.

Chapter 6

I laughed because he was drunk, but he was serious. If I had ever needed anything done on the low key, cousin Bone was the man. He could do anything you needed done and if he couldn't do it, then he knew of someone who could. He and Rabbit were always there for us all at Billy Goat Hill. No matter how they fought each other, they were there for each other. Rabbit always said that it was because they were brothers and if they weren't brothers, he would have fucked Bone off a long time ago. I didn't have any brothers, but those two were the closest that I had ever had.

Before I could say anymore, we both heard, "What the fuck y'all doing?" It was Rabbit as he walked where we were.

"Shit, talking," Bone said.

"Yeah, just talking," I said as I muffled back the tears that welled in my throat.

Rabbit grabs a seat next to me, and said, "You sound sad, Hog, out with it."

"No, I don't," I replied with a small laugh.

"Shit, you can say what the fuck you want. I have known you all your life and I know when something is up with you," Rabbit said.

"Rabbit, she said ain't shit up, so let that shit slide,"

Bone said.

"Okay, but let me tell you this. Don't ever cry over dick because it's a dime a dozen. Some is just better than others, but dick is dick all the same. Don't ever fuck off with broke ass niggas in the hood. Find somebody that will love you and, last of all, don't ever bring him to the Hill," Rabbit said. I laughed because that was so damn true.

"Awe shit, you done woke up the damn dreamer on the Hill," Bone said.

"What? You don't think love exists?" Rabbit questioned Bone.

"I'm not saying it doesn't exist; you just won't find it in the hood. You have to put your head in the books and rise above bullshit situations. Shit, Party is my sister, true enough, but she doesn't give a shit. She'll be hanging with mama 'nem forever. Shit, real talk," Bone said as he fired up a blunt.

"How you know?" I asked Bone to stop him from talking about Party.

"Look at it this way, she only cares about partying, getting high, and fucking old men. I love my sister and will fuck somebody up for her, but shit, to keep it real, you get out of life what you put in life. If partying and getting fucked up is all you want to do, then that is what you will get," Bone said.

"So, if I rise above these circumstances and come back for y'all, would you go?" I asked Bone.

"Hell no, because yo ass will carry me for so long," Bone said.

Rabbit and I laughed, and I said, "You just told me about getting in and out of life, and I may come back to offer you a better way of living and you say you won't take it. As for Party, that's my girl, you don't have to talk about her."

"It's only talking about her if I am telling a lie, but I am not lying. You know damn well your girl will get down and you know damn well I'll get down with her on Billy Goat Hill," Bone said.

"Party is not here to defend herself," Rabbit said as he laughed at Bone.

"Hog, all I am saying is that you have a head start to make something of yourself. Don't get your head full of water, and your damn belly swollen on bullshit and then have to get rid of it," Bone said.

"She hasn't done that yet," Rabbit said.

"Y'all tell me something. Why does Aunt Doll put up with Don's shit? I mean, he sleeps around and doesn't care who he hurts," I questioned my cousins.

"He eating her pussy, that's why," Bone said as we laughed.

"Naw, y'all know that Aunt Doll loves that shit," Rabbit said.

"Y'all wild," I said.

Rabbit, in a softer tone to imitate sounding like Aunt Doll, said, "Can't anybody take care of you like I do." Bone and I laughed because that was some shit Aunt Doll would say. "Aunt Doll didn't used to be that way," Rabbit said.

"Oh, for real?" I asked surprisingly.

"Yeah, Doll graduated the top of her class, went to college and everything," Bone said.

Interrupting Bone and Rabbit, I said, "Is that where she met Don?"

They laughed at me. Each time one of them stopped laughing; they would look at me and laugh even harder. "What's so funny?" I asked.

"Hell no, Don was the damn cafeteria worker. That cunning bitch wasn't in school, he probably can't read, either," Rabbit said.

I laughed as I asked, "How she didn't know about my mama, Aunt Tee, and him?"

"Dogs don't give a shit who they fuck as long as they fuck. I should know, I'm a dog ass nigga myself," Bone said.

"This is how I know all about that. Your mama had him first, but they got into an argument, and they broke up. My stupid ass mama went over to his house to talk to him, for your mama right after you were born. I think he was mad about it. Anyway, he smoothed talked Tee into fucking and then Aunt Doll was the innocent one. When he met Aunt Doll, he didn't go by Don. He went by his real name Donald, so she had no idea that it was the same guy until she brought him to the house to show off the one, she was so damn deeply in love with," Rabbit said.

"When she found out, she could have left him alone," I said.

"I believed she wanted to but try telling your heart who not to love and we can talk about it," Bone said.

That was some deep shit. All that time I assumed that Aunt Doll was a slut, but the truth be known she wasn't. Her life circumstances with Don made her to be the way she was. *It is the environment we are in and what we do in it falls back on us*; I thought. "I plan to get the fuck off Billy Goat Hill and out the hood," I said.

"Wait a damn minute. What the fuck is wrong with the Hill?" Rabbit asked with a smile.

"Look around this bitch. Everybody has been fucking the same dick or pussy for years. Shit, it's time for somebody to break the damn whore cycle," Bone said.

"Whore cycle?" Rabbit said as we both laughed.

"Peep this shit out. Name one person in the hood that doesn't fuck Don other than Party? Now, name one person that hasn't fucked Aunt Pan, Mama, or the Gutta Sluts?" Bone said.

Like fools, Rabbit and I both began thinking, and we could not think of anyone until Bone said, "Hog, you are the only person in the hood that is still innocent from all this shit."

"Huh?" I asked.

"You don't fuck Don, Big Z, Skeet, Legg, and that perverted as Cousin Po Boy. You stay clear from having a sugar daddy in the hood," Bone said.

"Yeah, you right, since you put it that way," I lied dryly.

"That is even more reason for you to get out, if you can," Bone said.

"Shit, if I had known what I know now, I would have stayed gone when I did leave," Rabbit said.

"Your bitch ass can't leave those Gutta Sluts alone and you can't leave those other community bitches alone, either. You always have to go fuck somebody in walking distance. You a dangerous bastard when you are alone," Bone said.

"Shit, I know you're not talking. You fuck them, too, and you even got a baby on the way," Rabbit said as he laughed at Bone.

"See, shit like that makes me get the fuck up and leave y'all alone. You can't pour a baby out this dick head. She might be able to drink it out, though," Bone said as he got up to leave.

Rabbit and I laughed at Bone, for he always talked nasty and about some girl blowing him off or doing something in that manner. If he didn't talk nasty, it wouldn't be Bone.

"Yeah, I better get up and go to bed. I'm glad that you are not as sad as you once were, Hog," Rabbit said as he got up and started walking toward the back of their house.

"Rabbit, I'm glad I got a chance to talk to you and Bone. I feel better," I said.

"Well, whatever it is, just remember, it could have been worse. Goodnight, Hog," Rabbit said as he walked out of ear shot of me telling him goodnight.

I opened the back door and stepped into the kitchen. I turned around and locked the back door. Mama said, "You saw us, didn't you?"

"Mama, what are you talking about?" I played crazy.

"You know exactly who and what I am talking about," she said as she got off the couch and came toward me.

"Mama, can we please talk about this in the morning?" I asked, for I was tired.

"Yeah, don't you leave this house until we do talk," she said as she went to her room.

I went to my room and got in the bed. I wasn't nauseated or anything and for that, I was glad. I replayed the entire conversation I had with my cousins and thought, *I am better than my situation and I am better than circumstance. I must get off the Hill and stay off the Hill.* I turned over and went to sleep. I wasn't in a deep sleep yet, when I heard Mama's voice.

"Wake up, Hog, we need to talk."

I turned over and saw Mama sitting on my bed. She came in before I could leave. Just by the look on her face, I knew it must be serious because she was in my room and, more importantly, she was sober. In fact, she had been sober a lot lately and that was weird. I sat up in the bed, and spoke, "I'm listening."

"You can't love Don because I love him. I always have and I always will," she spoke nervously.

I was puzzled for a moment, and then I responded, "Who said I love Don?"

"He says you do, and I know you do. I see it in your face when his name is spoken. I see it when you look at him, for you think no one else is looking, but I see it. I know you love the way he touches you and that, I can't have. I've had to play number two in his life for too long and I will not be out done by my own damn child," she spoke seriously.

"Mama, are you okay? Where is all this coming from? Do you need five dollars on a hit?" I asked to throw her off the subject.

"Hog shut the fuck up and listen to me for once in your life."

"You the one doing a lot of talking about Don and shit, I personally think you need something to calm your nerves."

"It's not about calming my nerves. It's about Don and

how much I love him. Are you not fucking listening to me?" she spoke as her voice elevated.

"I didn't say you didn't love him."

"But you do, and you should know that he will never want you, no matter how tender and young you are. We have been together off and on for a lot of damn years. I let my baby sister have him for a while and all these other sluts, but that ends today. Hog, back the fuck up off Don because you don't want this angry bitch on you," Mama said.

I looked at her because I had never her act so defensive over a man. Too many emotions ran through my mind and none of them could understand the new attitude Mama had. Therefore, I said, "Mama, you don't have to worry about me latching on to Don or anybody else in the hood. I am young, beautiful, and have a lot going for me, and as soon as I graduate this May, this bitch is bouncing like a ball."

"Hog, I don't think I have been completely honest with you, so let me explain. Who the hell do you think taught Don how to fuck? Me. Who the hell do you think was his first love? Me. Who the hell do you think he keeps fucking no matter who he's with? Me. Who do you think he talks to when he is down? Me. And who do you think he buys stuff for, and I don't mean just drugs? Me. No bitch in this hood or anywhere nearby can hold a candle to me when it comes to Don. If I want, I get, and Don will make sure of it. Why else do you think my sisters don't talk to me much? It's because of Don. They knew the history that he and I had long before you were ever thought about. They saw the love and mainly the money he gave me, so they got in on it and he started fucking them. Shit, I couldn't get mad, even though I wanted to. He started fucking them after you were born. He saw that you weren't his and he freaked, and guess what? So, did I. If I had known that you weren't Don's, I would have pissed your ass out. But, this one, I know is his," Mama said as she pats her stomach.

"You're pregnant?" The words stuttered out.

"You damn right and I'm keeping it," Mama spoke proudly.

"Who all knows?" I asked as I felt weak.

"You and Don for now. That is why we were celebrating in the shed. We would have come to my room, but Willie acted like he wouldn't leave, so I left out the house," she said with a smile.

I couldn't say a word. I wanted to hit her, but for what? Probably because of my fucked-up life. If it weren't fucked up then, it was now. I felt like falling out and not waking up. I wanted to run, but my feet wouldn't let me go. How could one ever compete with years of love that she has had with Don? How silly was I to think that a seasoned vet in the streets would love someone like me? Mama was only telling me how she felt without knowing that I, too, was pregnant by the same man. I gathered my thoughts, and said, "Now that you have talked, it's my turn."

Before I could tell her that I was pregnant, she said,

"Hog, I love you and have never asked anything of you. It's just that Don has been the only man that I have loved, and to know that my daughter loves him hurts me deeply. I never meant for any of this to happen. If Don had been your father, all this whoring would have been avoided. I was strung out on drugs when I got pregnant with you but with this one, I had decided to go after the man I had always loved and to have a family by him. I'm sure you understand why I am telling you what I have."

"Mama, I'm happy for you and if you want Don, go for it," I said.

I went in my room, put my face in my body pillow, and cried like never before. I would wake up and go back to sleep crying. I had never known that love had so much pain. I was exhausted and my eyes were dry from crying so dam much. I knew Mama loved him but had no idea that it was to that extent. She loved him and to see how drug free she was meant more to me than my love for him.

I planned to let him go and after that conversation, and there was no way I going to bring a child into the world. It was bad enough that my life was fucked up, why would I fuck up a baby's life? Plus, I would be so ashamed around the hood for people to find out that me and my mama were pregnant by the same man.

Days later, I awoke to the sound of someone beating on my window. I vaguely got up and when I did, I saw that my girl was back, along with Isis. I smiled at them and got up. It felt good to see Party, but at same time I didn't want to talk to her. There I was pregnant and must have an abortion soon, but don't have a clue how.

"Girl, you finally brought your ass back," I spoke to Party as I hugged her. I gave Ice a hug, too, and spoke, "I heard about your accident. Glad you didn't get hurt."

"Naw, it just shook a bitch up, though. You know I'm a soldier," Ice said.

"Yeah, we out here grubbing at Mama's. It's not like you to be sleep this time of day, you coming over?" Party asked.

"Yeah, let me get dressed," I spoke to Party.

"Well, y'all can stand here and chit chat, but I am going to get some more grub. My stomach is still growling like a motherfucker," Party said as she left out the room.

Ice was about to leave when I touched her hand. She said, "Party, I'm going to wait here to make sure Hog brings her bitch ass on. You go on and don't let them eat all the pecan pie up."

"I'll try, you just put your ass in hurry up," Party said as she left us alone.

Closing the door, I locked it, and Ice said, "What's up?"

"I need to talk to you, but I don't need anyone to know but you. I don't even want you telling Party. This is very important," I said as I stared Ice in the eyes.

"Okay, you can count on me although I don't know why all the secrecy is for. This must be deep because you don't want Party to know. Spill it," Ice said.

Taking a deep breath, my nerves shook as I said, "I'm pregnant."

Ice looked at me, stuck her index finger in her ear, and said, "What did you say?"

More calmly, I spoke, "I said I'm pregnant and Don's the father."

"You pregnant by Party's dad? That no good bastard with your Aunt Doll?" Ice said.

"Yes. The one and only. I don't know what to do, but I know for sure that I don't want this baby" I said.

Ice got off the couch and walked around the living room pacing. I didn't know what she was thinking because she did not talk, she only paced the floor.

"What are you going to do? I mean, how far along are you?" Ice asked.

"I found out Monday and I'm not that far along," I said.

"Shit, shit you don't have a whole lot of time to abort. I mean, that is what you are going to do, right?" Ice said as she sat down beside me.

"Yeah, but I don't have the money yet. How much will it cost?" I asked.

"To be done properly about five hundred dollars. How much you have?" Ice asked.

"About two hundred. You have any to help me out?" I asked her.

"I have about two hundred now, but I don't get paid until next week. We don't want it to be too late because the earlier we do it, the better. You don't want the fetus to have a heartbeat because if you do then, it is a form of murder, right?" Isis asked.

"Yeah, I already know," I said sadly.

"How you going to get the rest of the money?" Isis asked.

"Don't worry about it, it'll get done. Just don't tell Party," I asked.

"This is huge, and no way am I going to tell her that you are pregnant by her no-good ass daddy," Ice said.

"This is the first secret I am keeping from her, and it doesn't feel right. I hate this shit happened to me. What the fuck was I thinking?" I spoke to Ice.

"I know, but doesn't she know you fucked him? Did you tell him?" Ice asked.

"Yes, I did tell her about the first time and all I could see in her face was hurt. I promised myself that I would never hurt her. I promised not to fuck him again, but it was too late. I didn't even know I was pregnant."

"How you don't?" Ice asked.

"My period was on time, but lighter. Anyway, Monday I felt faint and sick, so the teacher sent me to the nurse, and she told me."

"I tell you what. You'll be six weeks when?" Isis asked.

"I don't know, but soon."

"That is enough time for us to come up with the rest of the money. I'll make you an appointment for Wednesday after school. Tell Party that you have something to do after school and you can't ride the bus home. I'll bring you home by saying that you were stranded and called me, but I was already on my way out this way for a surprise visit," Ice said.

"Okay, thanks so much," I said as I hugged Isis.

"Come on, we have to go eat and party tonight at the Gutta Sluts'," Ice said as she got up and waited for me to put on my shoes.

When we made it to Party's house, the food was still there and so were Don and Aunt Doll. I spoke to everyone and went on to the kitchen. We fixed us a plate and went outside to the tree in the front yard. We ate good but I was beginning to feel nauseated again.

"You, okay?" Ice asked.

"Yeah, just a little sick on the stomach again," I replied.

"You better straighten that shit up because Party will be out here in a few and so will everybody else. You are going to smoke a blunt or two with us?" Ice asked.

"Hell yeah, I can't let this baby stop me from having a good time," I said.

"You going to abort it, anyway, so what the fuck," Ice said as she ate her pecan pie.

"What y'all talking about?" Party asked as she grabbed a seat next to me.

"How we going to turn the party out tonight," I replied quickly.

"Hell yeah, I plan to get lit up and don't care what the hell I do," Party said as we laughed at her.

We chilled and I watched them drink wine coolers. I couldn't drink because that bastard inside me was making me sick to my stomach. I could barely hold it. I ran off and vomit in the woods close to where we sat. They all laughed at me, saying I was already drunk and how I couldn't drink all their shit up. I played along and even acted like I was too drunk. Isis even played along to make it look good.

It had gotten late, and I still pretended to be drunk just so I could lay the fuck down. Party went in the house, and Ice said, "Are you going to be, okay?"

"Yeah, while everybody at this party, I'm going to go get the rest of the money. If possible, make it for Monday. The sooner the better, I'm ready to be free of this sin I carry," I said.

"It isn't a party until the real Party parties, and she parties nonstop."

We looked up and Party was dressed to kill. She wore her new boots with a short mini skirt. Her hair was pulled back and tied about her head. Her shirt was short cut along with her jacket that came nowhere near her navel.

"I look good enough to eat, don't I?" Party said as she came closer to us with a big smile on her face.

"I don't know about all that," Ice stated.

"I got to lay this ass down," I said as I staggered some.

"Bitch, you going to be okay. You acting like you pregnant and shit. What the fuck?" Party asked.

"Whatever, I may come on down there in a few. Shit, I got to sober up first. Can't go to the party drunk, some bitch may jump stupid, and there I go getting a beat down," I said.

"Bitch, nobody is going to kick your ass, but yo ass is drunk so go lay that shit down and I'll tell you about it tomorrow," Party said as she turned to Ice.

"Come on, let's creep up on these whores and show

them how to party," Party said as she and Ice walked across the street toward the music that played loudly.

Everybody was gone and I stood in the yard alone. I went in my room and changed clothes. I put on a see-through shirt with no bra. I even squeezed my nipples so they would be hard and poke out. I put on a pair of thongs and a short pair of pants to reveal my long, slender legs. Stepping back outside, I needed to make sure that no one would see me walk toward Po Boy's house. I walked fast down the hill to my cousin's house.

Chapter 7

I had never been in her home, and she doesn't talk to us, anyway, so sleeping with her husband would be almost a treat for me. The closer I got to her house I felt nervous and fearful that someone would see me, but no one was around. Hurriedly, I knocked on the front door and no one answered. I was about to leave when the door opened, it was him. His eyes focused on my breasts as I knew they would, for my breasts were bigger since I was pregnant.

"Hey, why you ain't at the party?" Cousin Po Boy asked.

"I was, but I needed to make my own party," I said as I tuned my eyes to his crotch.

"What can I do to help?" he asked with a smile.

"Are you alone?" I asked.

"Yeah, she is gone to Vegas for the holiday to visit her sister. You know she's been sick and all. I'm sorry, come in," he said as he stood out of the way to let me in the house.

I walked in the living room, and it was elegant. It was far beyond my wildest dreams. She was right not to socialize with us because no one in the community had a home like theirs. The wrap around couch was spacious and looked comfortable. The tile was the most beautiful that I had ever laid eyes on. The room over all made me feel like I could have stuff like that and be somebody, for they had no children and were not suffering for anything.

"What can I do for you, Hog?" he asked with a sleazy smile as he raked over my breasts again and again.

"I need some money, and I know you have it, but you letting me get it, is another thing."

He smiled, and looks me up and down again and again, admiring my body up close and personal. I didn't like the way he smiled, but knew he had what I was in need of and that was money. Therefore, I pretended that he was someone I would desire so I would go through with the ordeal. I returned the smile, and said,

"I'm serious. I need some money, and I know you can help me." I waited on him to say something.

"Well, I can help you, but you don't have a job to pay me back."

"You know what I have and it's better than the money you want."

"Really? How do I know that this isn't a ploy to ruin me in the community or mess up what I have here?"

"Let me tell you this much, I already have a lot of shit on my mind and fucking up your home isn't one of them. Either you are going to help me or not?" I told him straight up, hoping he doesn't send me away empty handed.

He walked over and squeezed my breast, and my nipple got hard. "Tender, plump breasts. I like that. How much you need?"

"I need three hundred dollars," I spoke, hoping he wouldn't turn me down.

"You'll be worth it, I can tell. You see in this hood; I know who is doing what and I know that you are not out there like that cousin of yours. So, this is what I will do. I'll fuck you and if you hook me up with her, I'll give you one hundred dollars extra," he said.

"You have to pay her for her services, too," I said.

"She'll get hers; don't worry about that because I see the way she struts up and down the road shaking her ass at me. All I need is one chance and I will make her want me. Can you do that?"

"Yes, so what do I go?" I spoke.

He reached in his front pocket and pulled out the money. He handed it to me, and he said, "Follow me."

He took me to his basement, and it was nice. It had a bar, a big screen, a small fridge, a bathroom, and a magnificent bed. Nothing else caught my attention but the bed. I walked over to it and touched it lightly, for it was obvious that I admired it so. It looked like you could sink all the way to the bottom of it.

I got on the bed and immediately I wanted to sleep. That

was just how soft the bed was. It smelled really nice, and it was very inviting. I got up and took my clothes off, for I was ready to feel the sheets on my bare skin. I turned toward him, and he was already naked and waiting on me. Suddenly, I was so scared and never thought I would allow him to take what I knew he admired from a distance.

I didn't know what I thought, but he being gentle was not one of them. He was skilled and patient. Each move he made on top of me made me yearn for him. Maybe it was because I hadn't had any lover like him. Cousin Po Boy was slow and knew how to be a lover, unlike Don. Cousin Po Boy took his time to make real love to me, and I was amazed at how passionate he was. He didn't stop until I reached my peak, and, overall, I enjoyed sleeping with him.

When we finished, he said, "That was good. You can come here anytime you need some money, and this is our secret. So, don't go running your mouth," he said.

"You got what you wanted, and I got what I wanted. It was a win-win situation. Don't you agree?"

"Yes, I do. Come on and get out of here. I got to make sure no one sees you leave out here," he said.

I wiped off and we both went back upstairs. He went out the door first and no one was coming, so I walked out then he went back in. *That was the easiest three hundred dollars I had ever made, plus a hundred to hook him up with Party and it didn't take him long*, I thought as I walked back up the road toward home. When I got there, no one was there. I took a long bath and went to sleep.

The abortion finally happened just like Isis said and it made me have a different outlook on life, family as a whole. I began studying more and staying inside. Mama began showing and everybody wanted to know who the father was, but she wouldn't tell. I didn't feel jealous, but a part of me felt hurt because I aborted a child that could have been growing inside me. I was relieved that the ordeal was behind me, and Mama was acting like a real mama, in spite of her weird food cravings and bipolar moments. For the most part, I was happy.

From time to time, I would see Cousin Po Boy watching me and little did I know, Party fucked him and was sprung on that dick. He was all she talked about, and I could tell that she was falling for him, seriously. She was almost a changed individual and everyone on The Hill knew it. She boasted to me about where they went out to eat the previous night, and how he ate her pussy and fucked her slow. As I listened to my friend talk about a man, my mind wandered. I figured my girl deserved happiness, even if it was wrong.

School was out until the ninth of January, and I planned to chill out like I had been doing. Party had been too busy doing her thing and I was busy doing my school thing. Mama had quit leaving the house because of the baby and Don came over to see her almost every day. He really acted concerned for Mama and the baby. He would come over to read to the baby and talk to her stomach.

He actually looked like he would be a great dad, however, seeing him like that almost made me wonder if he would have acted the same way with me. I dismissed the thought quickly. I went outside and sat under the tree.

"Want some company?" Aunt Tee said.

"Sure, why not?" I spoke.

"My daughter is in love. Have you not noticed?"

"Yeah, I have, do you know who he is?" I asked so she would think I didn't know.

"That's funny, I was about to ask you who the man was," she replied.

"I don't have a clue," I said as I waved at cars that drove by.

"Who is he, Hog?"

"I don't know. Why won't you ask her?"

"I would, but she's gone almost every night. She's barely here and I know that you two don't hang out much," she said.

"No, we don't, but I respect her grind, and she respects the fact that I am trying to do my work more earnestly. As long as she is happy, why should it matter who the caller is?"

"It doesn't matter, I just want to know. That shouldn't be a problem with a mama wanting to know who her child is fucking, is it?"

"It's a problem if you bring him to The Hill because one of you will want to fuck him for his money, see the problem?" I said to her.

"Hog, despite how your mama did you, doesn't mean I will do the same to Party," she said.

I turned my head to her, and said, "What do you mean how my mama did me?"

"We all know that she told you to stay away from Don, and you did without calling her bluff. She is pregnant and it supposed to be his, but we all know that the father of that baby could be anybody's baby. Don better talk to DNA; while he keeps running up here trying to save whores and shit," Aunt Tee spoke as she puffed on her cigarette before saying, "Doll was up here all day today crying because she hasn't had kids by Don and her two sisters are having kids by the man she loves. That is fucked up, I admit, but damn, Pan didn't have to get caught up. She acted like Don loves just her. Just last week he loved Pinkie, when he was fucking the hell out of me, I guess he loved me, too, Hog," Aunt Tee said as she laughed.

"She's happy and if that is what she wants, then so be it," I said as I waved at another car that drove by.

"The shit is about to hit the fan."

I looked down the road to my right and Aunt Doll was coming up the road with a stick in her hand. I knew then that she was coming to our mobile home for Don. When she got closer, Aunt Tee yelled out, "Don't come on this Hill with bullshit, Doll."

"I'm not because the bullshit is already here, starting with that bitch behind you," Aunt Doll said.

Aunt Tee looked at me and I looked at her. I didn't understand what they hype was about, but if she wanted to get down and do the damn thing, then we would.

"Who you talking to?" I asked Aunt Doll.

"First, I am going to talk to you, then it's to that bitch sister of mine, your mama," Aunt Doll said with tears in her eyes and snot coming out her nose.

"Don is not my problem, he's yours and hers," I said.

"Yeah, you right because you fucked for money to get rid of a pregnancy," Aunt Doll said.

Aunt Tee looked at me, and I yelled out, "You lying bitch, shut that hole in your face before I put another hole where your eyes used to be. You don't know a damn thing. So, mind your own business," I said as Aunt Tee stood between us.

"Move out the way, Tee, I need to teach this trick a lesson," Aunt Doll said.

"I'm not moving any damn where, go home, Doll. You are not going to leave him, so go home and sober up," Aunt Tee said.

"I am sober and in my right mind. I'm fed up with her and her mama thinking they can steal the man I love from under me and be happy. I'll die and go to Hell today before I continue to be a door mat," Aunt Doll said.

Without thinking, I ran around Aunt Tee and smacked Aunt Doll in the face. She fell back on the cactus. Aunt Tee tried to hold me back, but she only had my shirt. I didn't want to hit my aunt, but it was one of those days that she caught me in a wrong mood. All the pain I had been feeling was released and I didn't hold back. I thumped her face and body as hard as I could because I was bitter and angry on the inside. She fought back, but not enough to keep me off her ass.

In my ears, I heard police sirens and people talking, but I didn't care. Rabbit finally pulled me off Aunt Doll. I had my back to her while Rabbit and I were arguing about how silly it was to hit a family member, but what happened next stunned me. Aunt Doll got up and busted me in the head with a palm size rock. The last thing I remembered was falling on Rabbit.

I tried to open my eyes. My head was banging real bad and all I could hear were voices in the background. The female voice sounded familiar, and the male voice was new. I stirred in a comfortable bed. I heard a man say, "Whoever Willie Jeffers is, he is not your daughter's father because his blood type did not match, but her blood type did match to a Donald Myers. We ran both of the men for her blood transplant and it's a perfect match to Mr. Myers. He is the father of your daughter," he explained.

"Are you sure? I mean, years ago they said he wasn't and now that she needs a blood transfusion you tell me that he is her father," the woman's voice said.

"Yes, our technicians ran the test three times, and the results were the same. We are sorry about that, but that was not a mistake done on our behalf. Here is your copy for court if you desire to petition for child support because she is still in school."

"Thank you so much for changing my life, doctor," the woman said.

"We needed blood and, luckily, this man gave blood," the man said.

"How could this have happened? All her life I told her that her father was one man now I find that it is another," the familiar voice spoke weakly.

"The compatibility is similar, and it is easy to make a mistake, I can assure you, but as of now there is not a mistake here," the man said.

Who are they talking about? I thought as I reached up to touch my head. I noticed that it was bandaged up and ached terribly. I tried to open my eyes, but the light hurt them so, immediately, I closed them and turned over to the other side. I felt a gentle touch and wanted to see who was touching me, but the light made me rethink.

I had no idea how I got there and what happened.

Slowly I opened my eyes, anyway, and to my surprise a woman was standing by a chair. She was plump and had tears in her eyes. My expression must have told her that she was a stranger because she said, "Hog, it's me, your mama, Pan."

I felt my face frowning as I continued to stare at the strange woman. I opened my mouth to talk, but words would not form so I closed it instead. The woman rubbed my hair and kissed my head before she said, "You're going to be okay, my daughter, you're going to be okay. I love you and I am so sorry you got hurt. Please, forgive me, please, forgive me. I didn't know."

She left, I closed my eyes, and then someone else came in. It was a girl. She looked to be holding back tears. I frowned at her, and she smiled, and then cried. Her mixed emotions had me confused. I didn't know how to take her appearance, but I only watched her. She walked closer to the bed, and I continued to gaze at her face for it seemed familiar, but not really. She sat down next to me, and said, "It's me, Hog."

Hog? I thought. *Why is she calling me an animal?* I asked myself. She must have sensed my confusion, so she rephrased it.

"I'm sorry, Mahogany, it's me Patricia, you know, Party," she said. I opened my mouth to speak, but nothing would come out. She went on to say, "The doctors say you may not remember much, but that is okay. I will fill in the blanks for you."

She handed me a notebook and a pen. I assumed she wanted me to write questions or whatever down I wanted to know. I stared at the paper and pen because I wasn't sure that I could read or write. I lifted up my hand to grab the pen, and I did. I tried to write, but it was scribble scrabble. *What's wrong with me?* I thought. I raised my hand and pointed at the mirror because I needed to see what I looked like.

The girl said, "Mirror. You want to see a mirror?"

I nodded my head yes. She got up, pulled the retractable mirror off the wall, and brought it over to me. I couldn't hold it well, so she placed it in front of me. I stared at the person in the mirror for a long time. I kind of recognized me, but for some reason I didn't. I made myself raise my hand to touch the mirror.

I traced my face, and the girl said, "Yeah, it's you, Mahogany."

I looked up at her and waited for her to speak more, but she didn't. Therefore, I said slowly, "Party."

The girl jumped up, and hollered out loud, "You remember me! You remember your best friend. We have so much to catch up and I know that this is all new to you as well as it is for me, but we will overcome this together. Tonight, I will party for the both of us, Hog. I mean, Mahogany."

I glared at her as she spoke, but no memory of us ever came to mind. Then, the doctor came in along with the plump woman whom called herself my mama. I could tell she was also very pregnant. The doctor said, "Ms. Jeffers, we are glad you came back to us. You have been out for a couple of weeks. We know that you may have some questions as to why you don't remember or why you are off key. You have a bad concussion which caused you to lose a lot of blood. The part of your brain that controls memory, speech, and writing was affected when you got hit on the head. This, to me, appears to be temporary and you could recover soon. However, speech could come back in a day or two. Some things you may remember quicker, some things may take longer, but if you continue on the path, you are on you should make a complete recovery soon. How soon is undetermined, however, some recover in a matter of days, some weeks, and others longer. Personally, from the looks of your brain, I would say a full recover in a matter of weeks."

He looked at the people that came in with him, and said, "May I talk to her alone, Ms. Jeffers?"

She agreed and they all left the doctor in the room with me. He came closer and sat on the bed. He stared at me, and said, "Ms. Jeffers, I asked everyone to leave because they don't need to know this personal information. Being that you are eighteen, you have the right to know this without a parent being present. You have syphilis, gonorrhea, Chlamydia, and a partial abortion. I would say before you got hit, but we went ahead and finished it properly."

I started crying, for I remember something about STDs, but to hear that I had more than one and not just that, a partial abortion had me going crazy. *What kind of monster was I before this accident?* I thought as I couldn't dry my tears.

"Ms. Jeffers, to begin with, luckily, we caught yours in time. You may not remember, but you must have had fever, bleeding, and pain in the lower part of your stomach. I hate you had this unfortunate ordeal, but glad you did because you could have died. As for your STD, you didn't have any symptoms; however, have you had any sores either around your mouth, pelvic area, or rectum that you can remember?"

I lay on the bed silently because I really could not remember anything at all. I tried, but nothing came to my mind.

"You can't tell us when you first experienced a symptom, so that makes it almost impossible to know how long you have had these STDs. I believe that whoever fathered your child may also be infected. We checked for any type of rashes and came up with nothing. Gonorrhea and chlamydia usually exist together, and I have to treat each disease differently. You should be thankful that you have what we call an old strain of gonorrhea because there are new strains out there that are harder to cure. Ms. Jeffers, it usually takes a single shot of penicillin and an oral dose. As for you being able to produce more children in the future, anything is possible."

The doctor stop talking as he waited for me to digest the information he gave me. In all honesty, I did not know how to take the information because I could not remember my life. Clearing his throat I thought, *there's more*. Soon as I had the thought, he spoke again.

"I wanted to know what type of student you were, so I had your mama to get a copy of your transcript. I am very impressed and hope you leave this lifestyle because you have a lot going for you and I don't want you to be another statistic when you can achieve higher. Go to college and rise above your situation. Put this behind you, learn from it, and do better. Okay? Shake your head if you understand all I have said."

I sorrowfully shook my head and sobbed. He got up, and said, "Good, I will dismiss you tomorrow for New Year's Day. A nurse will be here later to remove the bandage and tomorrow remove the IV. Ms. Jeffers, don't forget about what I said, okay?" I nodded my head as he asked those people to come back in.

They did and he said to the woman that must be my mama, "Ms. Jeffers will be able to go home tomorrow. Don't try to make her remember, it'll come back in due time. If she gets stressed, it may do more damage than good. Reframe from alcoholic beverages, nicotine, and sexual activity until you can make your own decisions. I want to see her back here in the next month to see how she is doing."

"What about school?" the pregnant woman asked.

"It depends on how well she recovers. As for now, she'll be out for at least another month or better, but that can change. I'm sure the school can accommodate her, so she won't fall too far behind," the doctor said.

Another girl came in and she seemed familiar. She smiled at me, and I knew I knew her, but I didn't remember her name or how I knew her. I felt kin to her, but that was it. I couldn't quite explain it, but it was like we had a connection. I almost smiled at her.

"Don't act like that, bitch" her tone was vulgar and offensive. I must have frowned, for she said, "I'm Ice. I mean, Isis, your distant cousin. Your grandmother and my grandmother are said to be sisters."

I continued to stare at the individual and, finally, I remembered talking to her and she was doing a lot of walking. I turned my head, and then I turned back to her, and said slowly, "Ice."

"That's me."

I could not say anymore because it was hard to say Ice. When she saw that I was not going to say more, she continued speaking. "You know, Hog, I mean, Mahogany I wanted to fuck Doll up, but we know she never meant to hurt you," Ice said.

"Doll?" I strained to say, for that name was familiar.

"Oh, they didn't tell you. Well, I won't tell you, for it may not be my place to tell you," Ice said.

I gave her a look and she before she was compelled to tell me, my room became bombarded by a lot of people. Many of the faces seemed similar and some were faces in a crowd. Two of the men's faces were very familiar to me. They came right over to me, and the shortest one said, "I'm Rabbit, your favorite cousin.

"I'm Bone, your other favorite cousin and his brother,"

the tallest of the two said.

"Rabbit, Bone," I said, for I remembered them well, bits and pieces of them at the most.

"Just take your time and recover, cousin. You have all the time in the world. I'm here. Tonight, I'll put one in the air just for you," Bone said.

What does put one in the air for me mean? I thought.

"Bone means that we are here for you and put one in the air means smoke a blunt for you because you are not going to be able to party with us," Rabbit said as if he read my mind.

"There you go trying to correct me and shit," Bone said to Rabbit.

"Well, somebody has to do it," Rabbit said.

"Don't start that shit in here," a woman's voice said as she came closer.

"Hey, baby, it's me," the woman said.

I said, "Aunt Tee?"

"Yeah, it's me. You, okay?" she asked me.

Chapter 8

I shrugged my shoulders because I wasn't sure how I felt. I closed my eyes because I wanted to sleep. The lady Pandora saw that I was getting tired and asked everyone to leave, and they did. I wasn't in the mood for trying to talk to anyone.

After everyone left, Pandora came over to me, and said, "Do you want to know about your life before the accident or not?"

Half of me wanted to know deeply, but a part of me didn't think I wanted to know about it. However, I nodded my head. I may not have wanted to know but felt that it was important for me to know about the old me.

"I used to be a drug addict. I would sleep with anyone for a little of nothing. I used to leave you alone all the time and sometimes, for days, you wouldn't even see me. Your daddy, whom I thought was your daddy, is named Willie. He is your uncle, my half-brother."

My eyes bucked. My daddy used to be my uncle, and I was a product of incest. I felt outraged as I looked at her disappointedly. She went on to say, "Yes, I got strung out on drugs at an early age and slept with him. Thanks to this accident, I found out your real father's name is Donald Myers. You call him Don because he goes with your Aunt Doll, the one who hit you. Speaking of her, she wants to see you. I had to see, first, if it would be okay with you."

I nodded my head. I wanted to see her, even if she was the reason why I was there. I felt no animosity for her or whoever gave me the STD. I looked at Pandora as she swallowed, and said, "We all fucked your daddy, Tee, Doll, and me."

"Uh." I thought all the sisters sleeping with the same man. *They cannot find anyone else to sleep with.* Disgrace for them all showered me. To think I was a part of that family made me sick.

"I know it sounds nasty, but to us it was tricking off, it isn't nasty at all. When you don't have what you need, you do what you must. Your real dad is back with me now and I'm almost five months pregnant. Your Aunt Doll has a new man from Hunter Ridge. There's no sense in telling you who he is because you won't know him right now because of your memory and all," she said.

How can she think that it's not nasty when they are sharing the same man? I hope this is a mistake and I am in the wrong family, I thought with disgust. I looked at her, and she said, "I'm pregnant by Don, who happens to be Party's father and your father."

So, I have a sister that happens to be my best friend, that's great, I thought. *Did I sleep with Don?* I wanted to ask as my heart began skipping beats. She must have read my mind, for she concluded, "Yes, you were in love with him, but that was before I got pregnant and before we knew he was your dad."

I started making gasping sounds because I could not believe that I screwed my own daddy. Out of all the men in the entire world, I purposely fucked my daddy. Was he the daddy of the child I aborted as well? Was I raped? Did he give me the STD? All kinds of questions went through my mind and I needed to see this, Don. So, I said loudly and as clearly as I could, "Don, I want to see Don."

Pandora nearly fell out her seat. She looked like she didn't want me to see him, but I had to. She didn't smile as she got up and went outside. Moments later, a man came in. He was tall, brown skinned, and, actually, not all that bad looking. Oddly enough, I could see our resemblance, even though I was brighter with brown eyes. I thought *how could these low lives not see that this man and I favored so much.*

He stood at the end of my bed, and said, "Baby girl, you asked for me? Are you going to be, okay?"

Soon as I heard him say baby girl, a light came on. I remembered how he entered me and made me feel so good. I remembered how I used to drink his nut and how he used to fuck me like I was his prize pussy. I remembered how I loved him and how he used to tell me that he loved me, too. My God, I remembered how he used to hold me in the air and thrust me harder than ever. By that, I meant he would screw me sore.

Yes, he was the first and last man I screwed because I

didn't have any memory of anyone else but him. He had to have been the father of the child I aborted, and he must have been the one that gave me the STD. *That nasty bastard!* I screamed in my head. I wanted to choke him, but he didn't know like I didn't that we were father and daughter. Suddenly, I started gagging and he handed me the small waste basket.

I vomited everything and then some. I continued to question in my head, *how is it that no one saw that we looked alike? How is it that no one cared to notice that we had the same physical characteristics?* Then, my mind said, "They didn't see because they didn't want to see it."

Tears flowed heavily down my face, and I could not believe what a life I had been living. I couldn't continue to live with those people, become a part of their environment, and end up like them. I just couldn't.

"Baby girl, I know what you are thinking, and I can assure you that it's fucked up. I had no idea that I was your daddy. If I had known, I never would have fucked you at all. Forgive me?" he said as he looked sincere.

I believed him, but the fact remained that we screwed. It was damn good, but bad. *How did I get in this mess?* I thought, but it didn't matter. What was done was done and nothing I did would ever change it.

"In case you want to know, only a few people know for sure that we had sex. That's me, you, your mom, and those two friends of yours, Isis and Party. I doubt they have told anyone about it, so your reputation is safe so far," he said. That made me feels somewhat better, but not too much better. I turned over and closed my eyes because hearing all that made me want to sleep. Don saw me growing tiresome. When he made it to the door, he spoke, "Get some sleep. You go home tomorrow. I promise to make things better. Please, forgive me."

I awoke to soft music playing throughout my room. It was nice and pleasant, the music I kind of remember hearing. It was soothing and pleasant to my ears. It made me think about all the stuff I had heard and how I had changed. When I opened my eyes, I saw a woman standing there. I knew that she had to be my Aunt Doll. She looked almost like me, but shorter, older, rounder, and lighter.

She came over to me, and said, "Hog, I never meant to hurt you, and I know you may not know or believe me, but I was angry and hurt. Can we ever put this past us and go on? Can you ever forgive me?"

I stared at her, trying to see if she was sincere, but a part of me really didn't care if she was sincere because if it had not been for her being angry, I never would of have noticed how jacked up this family of mine really was. I watched her facial expression again and that time I smiled. She broke down in tears. She came toward me and touched my hand.

Slowly, I said, "Yes."

Aunt Doll began to cry hysterically, and I remembered how she cried when she told Don to get out, but he left in her truck instead. She brought back a memory for me. That day I remembered seeing a woman truly in love with a man that did not love her back.

A few seconds later, Aunt Doll spoke, "I know you may not fully understand what I am saying, but I promise you that this will never happen again by me. Some things are better left unsaid, and often times those are the things that hurt us the most."

I touched Aunt Doll's hand because I feel that she was truly sincere. Because I couldn't remember, there was no telling the wrong that I had done to her or someone else. Oddly enough, something told me that I wasn't a bad person before the accident, but since the accident I was going to be a better person.

She gave my hand a slight squeeze, and said, "I'm dating someone new now. In the hood we call him Skeet, but his real name is Malcolm. So, I won't be around much because I am working and taking classes online to finish my bachelor's in social work. I will come to see everybody on the Hill. I decided that drinking and smoking wasn't the answer to my problem, Don was the problem. I've also decided to go into rehab to help myself. I have got to get out of this lifestyle, and you better do the same. Don't let the hood drag you down like they tried to do me."

Aunt Doll turned to leave, and then she turned back to me, and said, "When you get well, please, leave Billy Goat Hill. You are much better than that. You deserve the best. The Hill will make you a slut or whore, whichever comes first. I know I'm a living testimony."

Aunt Doll gave me a smile and walked out the door. I remembered when I was sitting and talking to Bone and Rabbit. I remembered how they said Aunt Doll was smart and to hear her leaving the mess made me proud of her. I took a deep breath and sighed. I was beginning to remember some things, and for that I was grateful that this unfortunate circumstance happened because my eyes began to open to the people I called family.

My speech had improved drastically from within, but not perfect. I smiled. As begin to drift off to sleep, a knock was heard at the door. It was the nurse. She came in and took off my head bandage. She spoke, "You're getting to go home today, Ms. Jeffers. What a way to start the New Year off by being a new you." She paused, stared at me to say, "Think of this hospital stay as a new you in the New Year."

I shook my head to agree because that was so true. I wanted to think of the year as a new me that would not be the riff raff I may have been before the stay. The nurse smiled at me. "Here are your follow up instructions. As you can see, no sex or alcoholic beverage until all this medicine is consumed. You are not to drive, but to get a lot of rest. Your memory will come back momentarily as the doctor described. Just use this opportunity to relax and rediscover who you are, and not what people tell you, you are."

I really liked the sound of what she said. She patted my foot, and said, "When your ride comes, have them to come to the nurse's station so I can wheel you out the front door. Again, have a great year, Ms. Jeffers."

The nurse smiled and left out the door. I sat up and got dressed in the clothes that Pandora brought. They were nice, but clearly not me. I had to wear them, anyway. Once I got dressed, I sat alone in the room, afraid of where I was going, better yet, afraid of not knowing where I was going.

I waited anxiously and nervously for someone to pick me up and after waiting three hours, no one came. I picked up the prescription and saw my supposed to be address. I pondered a little longer and noticed I had ten dollars in the small pocket. I pretended like my family was downstairs. I got the nurse to wheel me out to the front of Lackey Memorial Hospital.

"Where is your ride?" the nurse asked.

"They went around the back side to the ER," I spoke with humor.

"Well, I can't just leave you out here alone," she stated.

"There they come," I spoke hoping, she bought it and she did.

I got up and pretended to walk toward the car that was parked in the new parking area. She watched me for a few moments, then took the wheelchair back in and left me. I had never been so scared in my life of being caught and being thought of as a liar. Quickly, I went to the street and looked both ways. I had no idea where I was, but it all seemed familiar to me so I went to the left.

When I made it, the sign said Hwy 80. Remembering somewhat, I went to the left. I saw a Subway store and my stomach growled. I went inside and ordered a sub and a soda. She gave me the change and I sat down at the window. Before I could get into my meal, I noticed how a woman showered her children with affection. She talked to them tenderly and laughed, even her laughter was wholly.

The mother and her children sat down behind me, and the younger one said, "Mama, don't forget to order daddy's food."

"I already have it. You know I can't forget daddy's dinner," the mother said.

"Why his sandwich bigger than mine and my sister's?" the little child asked.

"Well, daddy works so hard, and he needs a lot more food to keep his body working. We don't want daddy to be hungry again and can't work, do we?" the mother said.

"Put your hand over your mouth when you talk. We don't want to see your food," the other child said.

"Settle down, children. We have to finish up so we can go see daddy at work," the mother said.

"Yes, mama," they both said.

"Don't tell daddy we were being bad in public," the

child spoke.

"I won't tell him because daddy has enough to do already. Let's finish up," the mother said gently.

I felt sad because from the way the mother was interacting with the children, I knew that I had never had that. It was funny for me to be sitting there thinking of family life and I didn't even know who I really was. I wiped the tears away because just by watching and listening, I knew something was missing in my life. Wrapping the sandwich up and closing the top of the bottle, I got up and walked out the store.

My heart was heavy, and my head began to ache. Not only did no one pick me up from the hospital, but I longed for positive family, not that group that came by to see me in the hospital. When I made it past the big church on the right, I stopped and looked around.

On my right was a grocery store called Sullivan's and in front of me was a tire shop. I remembered the girl I was with called him Poppa Bear. I remembered that was the girl that introduced herself as Patricia, but her given name wasn't that familiar to me, so I thought harder and remembered calling her Good Time.

Frowning, I knew that wasn't it, so I thought more and then the name Party came to mind. "Yeah, Party," I said out loud. But how close we were or things we had done would not come to mind. However, I remembered that the doctor said to relax, and the memories would come back to me. I started walking again and walked past the two graveyards.

Once I made it past the mobile home in the deep curve, I continued walking to the left and a car pulled up behind me. I stopped and a girl said, "Get your crazy ass in. I know you weren't about to walk to the country."

She was one of the girls that came to see me in the hospital. I was tired and I knew she knew where I had to go, so without hesitation I got in. She drove off in the direction I was walking.

"You know where you are going?" she asked me.

"No," I said with the shake of my head.

"Do you know who I am?" she said.

"I something?" I spoke.

"It's me, Isis, but Ice is my nick name, remember?" she said.

"Ice, tell me about me," I spoke slowly to pretend that talking was hard for me to do.

She looked over at me, and said, "You really don't remember anything?" I frowned and shrugged my shoulders to say no not really. She slowed down, and said, "You sure you want to know?"

"Yeah," I spoke with my head.

"You did have an abortion and the father is or, well, was

Don," she said.

I wanted to jump out the car because not only did I have an abortion, but it was by my father. *How did this happen? How did I get in this situation?* I thought as I cried.

"Don't cry, Hog. I mean Mahogany. You didn't know he was your father, none of us did, he didn't even know. He is Party's father, too. Now since I know you and Party, I don't see how we never saw the resemblance between you three," Ice said.

"Who all knows about this?" I stammered.

"Just you and I," Ice said.

"Does my father even know?" I asked.

"Yes, he does know. He does live with you and your mom now since she is pregnant by him and because he wants to spend time with you before you go to college, plus, she is having the baby in four months," Ice said.

"What about the brothers that came to the hospital to see me?" I asked slowly, trying not to let on that I could speak better than they thought I could.

"Oh, Bone and Rabbit? They cool enough. They are Party's brothers, your cousins like me, but they are closer kin to you than I am," Ice said.

We turned off Hwy 21 onto another street. Ice said, "Take your time and your memory will flow. Don't rush it, girl, it gone come back."

We passed by the Union Grove church on Old Jackson, and I remembered going out there a few times for funerals. Then, we went up a hill and I saw an abandoned looking car lot, and we went down another hill and I saw a small, paved road on the right. We went up a small hill and then onto a flat street. We didn't say anything. I just took in the scenery. She drove past a church called Mt. Hebron, and then I saw the water.

"Hold up, stop! Let me out of the car right now!" I yelled out as if I remembered something.

"Girl, what the fuck is wrong with you?" she said as she had a blank look on her face while pulling the car over.

I got out the car, walked to the concrete spillway, and stared at the water. It was calm and peaceful. The water was dark blue and appeared cold, so I took off my shoes and stuck my feet in. I closed my eyes, and a thought came to me of Party and me throwing little rocks in the water. We were talking about something, and then we got up and left.

I heard Ice yell with laughter from the car, "Its January, who in the world gone put their feet in some cold ass water?"

I turned toward her, and say slowly, "I just felt like it."

She walks toward me, and said, "You're not going to jump, are you? Because if you are, this bitch hasn't seen shit and this bitch hasn't heard shit."

Focusing my attention on her, I said plainly, "No, but

knowing what I do, jumping seems like the right thing to do right now."

I looked up and saw a fraction of a white house on a hill. It appeared depilated and worn, but with some type of promise. A piece of my memory came back to me that we all were up there hanging out, and somebody jumped stupid and got a gun.

"You thought about something, didn't you?"

"Yeah, who house is that over on that hill?" I said as I walked back toward the car.

"That is where your old girl used to live before she got evicted because she wouldn't pay rent," Ice said as she shook her head.

"Oh, for real? That sounds messed up," I said.

"Yeah, you know her and Don can't stay anywhere long without getting some shit started," Ice said as she walked back to the car and got in.

I put my shoes on and when she started driving again, we turned right on Billy Bay Drive. Seconds later, we turned into the driveway. The area appeared so quiet and void.

"Your home," Ice said as she got out the car.

When I got out, I went to the mobile home and put my bags up. It all seemed familiar to me somehow. I then walked back outside, and Pandora was standing in the door of the white house.

"Come here for a minute," Pandora said with a wave of her hand.

She moved out the way and the house were dark and quiet, so I turned on the lights, and people yelled, "Welcome home, Mahogany."

I was scared because I did not expect that. People gave me hugs and laughed. I did not know what to think. The faces of the people looked like I knew them, but then she came in, and said, "Welcome home, my home girl."

I knew then that she was Party. She threw her arms around me, and said, "Let's go outside under the tree." Anxious to see what she was talking about; I walked out with her. We went to the front yard and sat down. She lit some marijuana. I was appalled by it, and she looked at me oddly, and said, "I guess you don't smoke weed anymore since your little accident?"

I frowned in distaste. "Party, leave her alone. Let her take this time and allow her memories come back to her," a young lady said.

"Shit, you right. Sorry about that, Hog. I guess I thought since you remember some things that you would remember everything," Party said.

"Well, I don't mean to offend you or any of you, but I don't remember anything right now. It's coming back a little at a time," I said almost weakly.

"My name is Pinky, and this is my sister little, Yogi. Bone and Rabbit calls us the Gutta Sluts because we gutta and we sluts," Pinky said with laughter.

"I think I remember you two," I replied.

"Well, I hope you get your memory back. I'm sorry all this shit happened to you. Somebody needs to put a foot in Doll's ass. You know better than to hurt family," Pinky spoke with anger in her face.

When she said Gutta Sluts, I remembered them and the one talking, the younger Gutta Slut, always came and hung out with us. In fact, the last time she was over, she and I watched Bone and Rabbit fight. I remembered how Aunt Tee came out and made them stop.

Breaking my thoughts was Party saying, "Well more for me then."

"Yep, I ain't planning on smoking just yet, maybe not at all," I said, shrugging my shoulders.

"Damn, Doll must have knocked the fuck out you. You really don't remember shit?" Pinky said.

"What Aunt Doll did was knocked some sense into me and made me open my eyes to the kind of life I had been living. In fact, I was going nowhere fast and because of this, I know that now. Excuse me, I need to be alone," I said as I walked off from the group of females.

I went to the mobile home, and Party came behind me,

saying, "I'm coming, wait up, Hog."

"I'm not an animal and I do not prefer to be called that."

Then, Party said, mimicking me with deep emphasis, on Hog, "Well, wait up, Ma Hog any." I stopped walking and waited for her to catch up. She got next to me and I started walking again. "Look, Hog, I mean Mahogany. I'm really sorry. Things have been hectic since you been in the hospital and all. Shit, I'm sorry. I mean, dang, I miss us hanging out, walking, and talking. I hope you understand it. Now I know that we are inseparable you are my girl 'til the end," Party said with sincerity.

"Apology accepted. I just have to get everything back in my mind, that's all," I spoke as I made it to the front door.

"Mahogany not only are we best friends, but best of friends and no blood test will change that, my sister," Party said as she walked inside with me.

Chapter 9

I took out a knife, an apple, raisins, and peanut butter. I cut the apple in half and spread the peanut butter on it and added the raisins on top. I poured a glass of milk and prayed over my snack. Party glared at me funny, but I paid no attention to her. She sat at the kitchen table with me, and said, "Dang, Mahogany, you eating stuff like that now?"

I looked at the food, and then back at her before saying, "You mean I never ate this before?"

"Hell no, you never ate shit, I mean, stuff like that before. In fact, eating stuff like that was never in your vocabulary."

"Really, this is healthy for you. It's called ants on a log. Don't knock it until you try it," I said.

"Hell no, let me show you a hood snack."

She got a glass of milk and some Oreo cookies. She sat at the table again and began eating with her mouth open and smacking while she ate. I watched her dip the cookies in the milk and eat it. She sat there and I watched her as I ate my own healthy snack.

"Mahogany, now this is a real snack. Try one?" Party said.

"Only if you try one of mine first?" I questioned back.

Party took the slice of apple that was covered with peanut butter and raisins. She stared at it, and I said, "It's not going to bite you."

"Shit, it might as well hit me in the damn face, trying to get me to eat like white folks," Party said as she took a nibble of the snack. When she finished, she said, "Not too bad, but nothing I would eat as a snack. Your turn." I took the cookie and dip it as I saw Party do. It was okay, I just didn't remember ever doing it. "Well, you like it?" Party said.

"It's okay, but I like mine better because you get a serving of fruit and protein," I said.

"What are you now, a health guru?" Party said as she laughed.

"No, not that I know of, but I only have one body, and I have to take care of it," I said.

"Let me tell you what you have been missing," Party said.

"What I been missing?" I spoke.

"Listen, that night you got hit by Aunt Doll, I got in a scuffle with the police. They wanted us to move out the way, but I wouldn't leave your side. The policeman and I got in a tussle and down on the ground we went," Party said.

"Wow," I said, for I was surprised.

"Shit yeah," Party said as she paused, and then

continued. "Let me change the conversation for a minute. I don't know if I can stop my way of talking because you are a new person and all."

"Thanks," I said as I lingered on her every word.

"Anyway, I got sent to the detention center. Mama found out who the presiding judge was and as luck would have it, she used to fuck him back in the day. She paid him a visit, and they been fucking since then," Party said.

"How much time did you get?" I asked.

"I had to stay there for seventy-two hours, and then I was released to Mama. I came by to see you after court. I am on house arrest until May. See my black anklet?" Party said as she held up her pants leg to show me her monitor.

"Were you afraid?" I asked her again.

"No, not really because some of those tricks inside were all talk and shit, I was down for whatever," Party said as she looked at me.

"House arrest?" I asked.

Laughing, Party said, "Ha, funny you should ask."

By the way she said that I felt that she had done something underhanded. Looking at her, I said, "Who did what?"

"Didn't I say Mama used to fuck the judge and when she

found out that it was him, she rushed down and gave him some ass, and here I am," Party said.

"Okay, you learned your lesson?" I asked in an unsure way.

Party said, "Girl there wasn't shit to learn, I was being me, but you may not remember what being me is," she said.

"I'm sure it will all come back to me eventually," I said to assure my friend.

"Yeah, I know it will, but in the meantime, I'm about to go get drunk and fuck," Party said as she got up to leave.

"Well, I want to hang out here alone for a little while to gather my thoughts and possibly get some sleep," I said.

"Ok, I'll party enough for both of us, even though you weren't much of the partier," she said as she left out the door.

I closed the door and cleaned up the table. When I finished, I laid on the bed to rest. I could barely hear the music and voices as I closed my eyes. Deep down, I could remember a little bit, but I played dumb because I really didn't want to be a part of that world.

It was the first day of school and I felt like that was where I belonged. The people were nice, or maybe they were acting like that because I was hurt. Anyway, I actually enjoyed being there rather than where I lived. I saw Party around campus, and she was always hard. Maybe I was the same way because we hung together. Either way, I had no idea.

The people talked to me whenever Party wasn't around, for they seemed not to like her much. I don't know why, but they were all nice to me. My voice was back and, unfortunately, so was my memory, but no one knew that I had remembered everything.

It was the last class of the day, and I heard Party's voice ring loud in the class before I could get there. When I made it to the room, she was going off and cursing out our Spanish teacher in hood language. I tried to intervene, but it was too late. She had sent for the principal to come to our room along with security guards, trying to get the class under control.

Everyone in the class talked loudly and seemed to be on Party's side for some reason. The teacher looked afraid of the small group of students that were all talking. I rushed over to Party after fighting my way through the crowd of some instigating students.

"Calm down, Party, you don't need to get sent home. That is what they want," I said in a raspy voice.

"Shit, I needed to go to the bathroom and the bitch wouldn't let me. What the fuck was I to do? Piss on myself?" Party asked me and the other students directly that was standing nearby.

Some of the students said, "Yeah, Party right."

Others in our circle said, "She doesn't like blacks, anyway. Look at her, she has messed up now."

Tuning them out, I turned to say something to Party, but the principal had made his way over to us, and said, "Don't worry, young lady, you will be taking your bathroom breaks all next week at home. Let us go."

"What the hell is sending me home going to do? That's where I want to be, anyway," Party said in anger as the security guards toted her away to the office.

The teacher could not regain control of the class because they were not listening to her. People talked the entire class time. I was stunned because Party was sent home and from the looks of it, she wanted out of school, anyway. I felt sad for her because education was the only way off The Hill.

I got off the bus and went to the mailbox. I stood there going through the mail and saw that my report card had come. I was scared to see mine because for the last few weeks, I had been making up missed work from being out in December and keeping up with present work just to pull up my grades.

My hands shook as the paper envelope was in my hand. I was nervous about opening the paper, but confident all the same. Party was already at home, sitting under the tree drinking and smoking cigarettes. I stood at the mailbox and opened the letter from the school. I was surprised. I must be a lot smarter than I thought because my grades were not that bad. My report card had five A's and two B's, and the B's were plus' at that.

"Party, I got a good report card. What did you get on yours?" I spoke.

"Girl, I haven't even opened it because it's useless."

"Let me open it for you."

"Here, open it."

I opened it and looked at it. I saw two C's, and five D's. I looked back at her, and said, "Well, you'll still be graduating so far. You have two Cs and five Ds"

"Shit, I did have all Fs," Party said as she drank her beer.

I left from under the tree and went home. I went to my room and changed clothes. I didn't feel like hanging out, but I had to. I hadn't been near my mom or my father since I came home. I couldn't be around them, and I interacted with them as less as possible. I saw Party still under the tree, so I went back outside where she was.

Moments later, Aunt Tee came with Bone. She got out the car and was going off. "I couldn't believe that bitch case worker of mine."

"What she do?" Party asked.

"She had the nerve to ask me about my income," Aunt Tee said.

"How is that bad?" I asked pretending as if I didn't know. They all looked at me and started laughing. I had the idea what was so funny but said anyway "What did I say wrong?"

"Just because I don't have a job and I my bills gets paid, she wants to know how the hell things get done," Aunt Tee said.

I pretended to be puzzled because it made sense. *How would her bills get paid? How does she survive?*

"I had to go to the left on that bitch. I put her in her place. It was none of her business how I get my money, and her job is to give me my damn benefits. Shit, she better not mess up with our eating," Aunt Tee said.

"I was surprised she didn't go to jail the way she was cutting the fuck up in the welfare department. FPD will hull a motherfucker out in a minute. Shit, they crucial," Bone said.

"I wasn't going to jail because that bitch knows that I know who she fucking and if she fucks me up, I'm fucking up her home," Aunt Tee said as she lit a cigarette and sat under the tree with us.

Moments later, Cousin Po Boy came through. He honked his horn at us and drove off. I suddenly remembered him on top of me. He was going in and out of me, and my body responded to him. He was gentle and took his time sleeping with me. I had never experienced someone taking their time to enjoy my body. I had smiled a faint smile, and Party said, "I'm going to ride something tonight I see" She wiggled her ass in her chair.

I remembered her telling me something about going with him and how she was smitten by someone. *It must be him*; I thought as I saw her smile at the thought of the man that blew his horn.

"Party, you a little slut," Bone said as he drunk some beer.

"If I'm a slut, what do you think it makes you?" Party said to him as she picked up a wine cooler.

"A slut's brother," Bone said with laughter.

We all laughed at that, even Party, but she only mocked him by making faces. Aunt Tee went inside to cook.

"Guess I'll go down the driveway and see what the Gutta Sluts are talking about. Probably get a free drunk and some head in the process," Bone said as he walked across the road and into their driveway.

I saw my dad, Don, peeping out the window. He came out and started walking over to us. I didn't want him to come near me, but a part of me desired to be in his arms again. I found that I couldn't help myself, wanting the man that turned out to be my father.

Party said, "Our so-called dad is coming over."

"Hey, can I get one of those beers or wine coolers?" Don asked as he showed his white teeth.

"Don, is that all you want to have?" Party asked.

I looked over at her and she allowed her breasts to be exposed some. I got angry because he was my father and a man

I had loved. I felt uncomfortable and sick to my stomach that I still desired my own dad. Don looked over at me as if he could read my mind. He spoke softly, "Are you alright, Mahogany?"

"Yeah, I'm fine. Thanks for asking," I said as I drink some bottled water.

"That's good to hear," Don said.

"Don, is the business good?" Party asked as she licked her lips at him. I thought she was crazy because he was her dad, too. She never acted that way.

"Party business is always good with me," he said.

"Just checking in case, I need something. I'll get at you later," Party said as she smiled.

Don laughed and walked back to our mobile home. I looked over at her and she was still looking at him. I decided to check her, so I said, "What the hell has gotten into you? You do know that he is still your daddy, too."

"Bitch, the hood says that he might be my daddy. I don't fucking know if he is or not. You had blood test, not me. My daddy could be any one of these stray niggas out here in the hood. And, I have fucked about all of them. For all I know, I could be fucking my own daddy right now and don't even know it."

"You're full of it, Party. I don't think you should be trying to screw Don until you know for sure. The hood could be lying. Don just might be your real father," I tried to explain, hoping she would come to her senses.

"Well, to be honest with you, it's not what you think," Party said.

"You don't know if he is your daddy or not. Your mama says he is, and I believe her. I had him before I knew he was my dad and that was not my fault. I also didn't talk out of the way in front of you. I respected you enough not to do that in front of you. Give me some credit," I spoke as I turned my head away from her.

"True. Aight, I'm sorry. I'll respect you on that. We still girls? And, yeah, I know my mama still say he is my daddy. I don't believe she really knows who my daddy is," Party told me.

"Your mama has no reason to lie to you," I spoke.

"You are right, but your mama thought her half-brother was your daddy and it turned out to be somebody else. So, what the hell are you talking about? Those bitches were probably fucking everybody around here in the hood. Like I said, I don't know who my father is."

"You are right, but I wouldn't sleep with him until I knew for sure," I replied.

"Yeah, you are right." She sounded disappointed.

"Remember, no dick will break us up," I said, the lie she wanted to hear. In my heart, I knew that if she screwed him it was going to be her ass on the chopping block.

I excused myself and went home. When I got there, Mama was still asleep, and I was left alone thinking. I stared at the ceiling and fell sleep dreaming of Don. I began to remember nothing but fucking. My mind recalled the few times in my life I had been sexually active, but that wasn't enough. I was wanting more and was in need of more.

The way Don thrust me was heaven sent and the way I drank on him was pure bliss. A part of me needed to take him again, but another part of me needed to leave him alone because he was my father. Something was awakened inside of me as that side of me fevered Don.

I needed to feel him again. How ironic, I needed him. Don had been plain Don to me longer than he had been daddy to me. With a smile, I knew which side won. After tossing and turning because I was toiling in my sleep, I was drenched in sweat and aching to be penetrated by Don.

Getting up, I went to the kitchen and poured a glass of water. I slurped it down slowly. Some of the water eased passed my lips because the lamp came on. I heard, "You thirsty?"

I swung my head around fast to see my dad sitting on the couch. I thought I was alone, so I swallowed hard and gathered my thoughts. Putting the glass on the table, I squeezed my nipples, and faced him to say, "Depends what you think I am thirsty for."

He laughed, and said, "I saw you drinking water and assumed you were thirsty, that is all."

I walked slower toward him, wearing only my long muscle shirt that barely covered my ass cheeks. I sat facing across from him on the couch and crossed my long, slender legs so his imagination would take him up my thigh and to the G spot. I saw his eyes following my legs all the way up to my breasts.

He saw they were on hard, as he now swallowed harder to keep his attention off me. I lifted my leg up, twirled my foot around as I pointed it at him, and said, "Shouldn't you be in bed with Pandora, holding her and the baby she carries, which may not be yours, anyway?"

"It may not be, but you don't call her Mama anymore?"

"Enough about Pandora," I said.

"Oh, okay. It's Pandora now? What's on your mind, Mahogany?" Don said with a smile.

"Do you really want to know what is on my mind, Don?" I spoke coyly to him.

He laughed. "You sound like you are the shit, baby girl," Don said as he sat up on the couch with his hands entwined, patting his foot on the floor lightly.

"You are funny, and I bet you used to be in control of everything, right, and everybody's body, right?" I said as I made my breasts move. *Yes, he's watching me like a hawk*, I thought as I smiled more.

"Yeah, I do control the situations I get in," Don said as

he watched me come closer.

"Well, not today. In fact, no more of you being in control," I said as I stood up and rolled my hips the way I used to when we did fuck.

"My, my, my, Hog," Don said with a shaky smile.

"No, call me Mahogany because you love that, don't you?" I spoke as I stood in front of him.

"Damn, that hit on the head has brought out the bad girl in you, my little temptress," Don said.

"It did more than what you think," I said as I allowed him to put his hands on my hips and move with my rhythm.

Quietly, he said, "I can't do this. You are my daughter. God, you are so beautiful."

I slapped my ass in front of his face and responded seductively, "Right now, I'm just plain ole Mahogany and no one has to know."

"I can't help it," Don said as he watched me in front of him.

For the first time that I could remember, he licked my ass and moaned lightly. I could not tell if it was good or not because I was so preoccupied with making him want me. He acted like a dog eating hungrily. I removed myself and he lingered after me.

I smiled, and said, "You know, I used to have that same look when you played me and before long, you will crave me and the goodies I have."

I walked on to my room, and he was still on the couch watching peeps of my ass as it went in and out of sight from him. Before I closed the door, I bent over and gave him one last view. Looking between my legs, he licked his lips, and I laughed as I closed the door.

Lying on the bed, I was profoundly thrilled of the new Hog and all her memories. I also found delight in my conniving way to fuck my way to the top of the game. I smiled, and for the first time in a while I went to sleep with a plan and a vengeance.

"Hog, wake up," I heard Pandora's voice on the other side of my bedroom door.

"Yes, I am awake," I spoke as I am not getting used to being called an animal.

"You going to school today, aren't you?"

"Yes, I can't learn anything at the house," I spoke as I got up.

"I'm leaving out this morning. I have to stay overnight in the hospital. They are going to monitor my baby's heartbeat," Pandora said.

"Okay, I'll be alright until you get home," I said.

"Are you sure? Don will be here if you need him. And

don't go getting no ideas, he is your daddy," Pandora said.

"Okay, I know he is my daddy. I'll more likely stay at Party's tonight," I said as I smiled persuasively.

I heard her feet move away from my door and I immediately began to plot on what to do. When I walked up the hall, I saw the bus go down the hill. I looked out the window and saw no one stirring. I knew Party was not going to school and there was no way that anyone would know if I was there or not. I saw Cousin Po Boy wife's ride through in her shiny new Mercedes, and I knew that the real game was about to begin.

Showering and putting on my two-piece bra and panty set under my lace shirt and skirt. The bus left out and I made sure no one was looking before I walked down the road. I went straight to Cousin Po Boy's house. I knocked on his door and he opened it with a smile. I smiled back, and said, "I saw your wife leave and knew that you were lonely today and am in need of some loving."

Smiling, he let me in. His eyes covered me up and down as he said, "What makes you think I need some loving today? Plus, I thought you had some type of memory loss or something."

"I know exactly what I'm doing and what goes on around here," I told him, hoping he wouldn't say a word to anyone. He probably wouldn't because he didn't want people to know he was fucking me, too.

"Now, why do you think I want you?" he asked again.

"I'm young and tempting, what man don't want some loving from someone like me?"

He went outside and put his car in the garage so anyone that came by would think he was gone. I liked the way the house was decorated and to be honest, his wife had great taste. Looking around, I noticed that no family pictures were on the wall and the house seemed lifeless. She could not have children, and he did not have any that I could remember.

What I did see were pictures of them on exotic vacations and various escapades. They had an appearance of being in love, happy, and full of laughter and fun. *What a front*, I thought as I saw them pretending to be happy. He came back inside, locked the door, and said, "You like the pictures of us?"

"No, not really because it is a front, you know, a fake," I replied.

"What makes you think it is a front or fake?" he questioned.

"If you were as happy as you appeared to be, then you wouldn't be here getting ready to dog fuck me," I spoke as I took off my lace shirt.

He smiled and chuckled a little. "That doesn't mean that I am not happy. It just means that I like a variety in my life. I get bored easily."

"Variety or not, you either going to let me blow your mind or you are not," I said as glared at him deviously.

"So, you plan to screw me in my house? Where I live with my wife?" he said with a smile.

"I'm going to fuck you all over this house and every time you are here with her, you will be reminded of me and oh what a smile you will have," I said as I unzipped my jeans.

Chapter 10

He sat back on the couch and in my head, I heard dance music. I silently began to do a strip tease for him. Cousin Po Boy really enjoyed the show I put on for him. Every move I made toward him made him reach for me, but I would back away and dance out of arm's reach of him. When I pulled off my bra I threw it on the side of him, and he picked it up and sniffed it with a smile.

My breasts jiggled all over the place and I knew he loved my lovable sized breasts. I got closer to him and allowed him to bury his face in the valley of them. When I removed my tits, he wiggled his head side to side. The nipple brushed against his lips, and he grabbed it in his mouth. I gently pulled it out his mouth, and he said, "More, more."

I played peek-a-boo with my thongs to him. "More, I want to see all that firm ass of yours." I pulled my thongs off and threw them at him. He smelled them, put them in his mouth, and spoke softly, "There's nothing like the smell of young, hot pussy in the morning."

I took off my skirt and lay on the carpet with my legs spread. He got on his knees and began licking my pretty pink pussy. He was slow, and that intensified the foreplay. I got up, and said, "You can't eat it all in one serving."

"Like hell I can't. Lay your ass down and let me show you that I can," he said as I sat in his wife's chair and placed each leg on an arm.

Like a beggar, he ran over to me and tongued fucked me like a champ. If I was naïve and old Hog, I would have been blown by now, but I was the shit and the new Hog was the fuckee, not the fucker. I grabbed his hair and pulled his head up from between my legs. He looked surprised at me. I spoke, "Stand up and let me make you fall to- your knees."

"I'm young and if I need to take something for a younger thang like you, I will," he said.

"Hope your heart can take the ride because the amusement park doesn't close if you get sick. It moves on to the next rider," I said as I watched him take off his clothes.

While he undressed in front of me, I checked his body out completely. He was not a bad looking guy naked. His ivory looking skin tone and misty eyes did make him a looker, but he was just as much as a whore as the next person. I began to tease his penis with my tongue and tenderly squeezed his balls. Cousin Po Boy moaned and wiggled his legs.

"You like that?" I asked, for I already knew he did.

"You can't talk with your mouth full," he responded. I smiled.

I traced his dick with my tongue ring and his legs shook. I plopped the massive dick in my mouth and went up and down on him with passion. Taking my time, I tightened my lips around the head of his dick as I pulled up on him. He embedded my head deeper into his gray and black hairy crotch. I then removed his hands, and said demandingly, "I didn't tell you to touch me."

"I'm sorry. I'm sorry, keep going," he whispered as he took his hands off me.

Tasting him again, I went up and down a few more times, whisked my tongue ring around on his dick, and went faster to entice the moment. Pulling away from him, I got up and he said dryly, "What are you doing?"

"You have to follow me to continue the game," I said as I got up and went in the kitchen.

I had lain on the bare table and opened my legs. He tasted me hungrily, but little did he know I wasn't interested in having an orgasm. I only used him as a toy to start my fucking up shit plan. When I saw that he was getting carried away, I pulled his head up. He grinned, and said, "You got to let me finish tasting you so you can taste me back."

"No, not yet. We have all day, and I intend to make memories for you in ever y part of the house," I spoke as I got up and went to the sitting area.

It was there that I had him to bend over, and I began to lick his ass. He talked out his head as I went from his balls to his ass. From time to time, I would stop and beat his dick, but I always went back to the licking and sucking of the ass and balls. Finally, I got up, and he spoke, "Hog, I can't take too much of this play shit. I need to feel some hot, tight pussy."

"Shush. You eager for it, then come get it," I said as I went in the guest room.

I got on the bed on all fours, and he got behind me and replied, "Now, this is what I been waiting for."

He entered me and began humping me in a fast pace. I knew he really must have taken something so he could nut again if need be. The more I worked my ass on his dick, the more he grunted and tried to go deeper into me, but I couldn't let that happen. I fell flat on my face, and he slid out me.

"Come on, I feel that nut. It's right there," he said.

"I know, but what is the hurry?"

He grinned.

"You have changed since the accident. I never would have thought that you would be giving me the pussy like this," he said as I got up and he walked behind me with his dick in his hand.

I went to the basement, and there I got on my back, and said, "Come get that nut, but grind it slow so you can feel every time I throw it back to you."

He hurriedly climbs on top of me and was inside me. I tightened my legs around his back so he could feel every inch of my pussy. He made love to me like I was his wife, but I was a bitch and wife material was not in my vocabulary. The more he grinded, the more I allowed him to lose himself in me. He talked about how much he loved my pussy and how he wanted to buy it all from me. I could only grin to keep from laughing. His eyes were closed, and he was all in it, but I wasn't. I only watched him as he tried to give me his all. Before he started to cum, I said, "Get up for a minute."

"Hell no, I feel that nut, it's not going to wait."

I smiled and bucked him off me. He was stunned. "Get your ass on the carpet so I can get that out you."

He obeyed me and soon as he got on the floor, semen began dripping from his long ass dick. I took my finger and touched the slimy specimen. Kneeling beside him, I took my tongue ring and mobbed around the tender head of the dick. He was shivering as if he was cold, and I began drinking from his dick like a straw. His body was on fire from the heat I gave him.

Cousin Po Boy didn't know what to think because I took him to another level no one had ever taken him. I could tell that this type of kinky shit was not a joke. He got the full effect, for I wasn't there to play with him, either.

"Hog, here comes that nut, here comes that."

He couldn't finish his sentence, and he didn't have to warn me, for I already knew what was happening to him. I moved my mouth, and his nut went all over my face and breasts. Cousin Po Boy started breathing hard and staring at me like I was a prize. Grabbing the nearby shirt, I wiped my face and mouth off, and softly spoke, "Get up and bring your ass upstairs to me."

As weak as he was, he followed me slowly. Each area I walked in from the living room to the kitchen, I remembered how we fucked, for I wanted him to remember as well. I stopped in the hall and sucked his dick, and like a charm he was hard again. I jumped up on him and he held me in the air for a second, long enough to slide that dick in me. Even in the air, I worked that dick like a pro until he came again.

When I felt like he couldn't go on, I would suck him to get him hard. The final act was when I lead him to his wife's bed and jumped up and down on his dick. The more I worked my ass and back, the deeper I worked his dick between my thighs. I turned around and gave him a perfect view of my ass. When I dropped down on his dick, I noticed his toes spreading as his legs shook while I rode him backwards.

Switching positions, I faced him and allowed him to see my breasts dangle in front of him. Whenever I worked my ass to one side, he begged me to stop, but I couldn't. I was in my zone and had to let him know that I was going to be the bitch that ran this hood. I stopped, and then I worked my pussy all the way to his balls and bounced up and down. He is getting pure pussy and nothing else.

"I can't take it. Stop, Hog, stop the pussy too damn good. Get up, let me rest, get up!"

"Not until you give me one last nut," I said as I worked my ass slower to let him feel the full effects of the sex I gave him.

"Here it comes," was all he said as he tossed to and from under me. He tried to shake me off, but I had my legs locked under him.

I got up and sat on his face, and he licked my pussy clean. I had a dry orgasm, but it mattered not to me. Seconds later I got up, for Cousin Po Boy was unconscious, naked, and fucked down by me. *Damn, I fucked him to sleep*, I thought as I smiled.

"Get up and get in the bed."

I said as I went to take a shower. About ten minutes later, I came out dressed. I checked the time. I didn't even hear the bus come; topping it off I could not believe that I had been there all day and half the evening fucking that bastard. I knew that I did my job. I peeped in and he was still sleep, but under the cover and snoring.

I heard his cell phone ringing and saw that Party was calling. I knew she wanted to fuck off with him for some money, but the early bird gets the worm, and late comers get what was left. I laughed because she was gonna have to get up early in the morning to beat me. Pressing the button to ignore to her call, I laughed again.

Party looking out the window as I approached the driveway. She walked to the door, and said, "It's really late. Where have you been and why didn't you get off the bus here?"

"I got off down the road because I hadn't ridden the bus in a long time. Then I went through the woods and thought about how we use to run and play there. I didn't realize how quick time had gone until it started to get dark some" I lied straight in her face and didn't care.

"Oh, well, if you had waited until next week, I would have done it with you," she said.

"Give me a few minutes and I'll be out. I have to change clothes."

When I went in the house to take off my clothes, I heard, "I plan to fuck the shit out of you, daughter or not. I got to have that tender, hot ass one last time."

"You better get ready because this pussy isn't free like it used to be," I said as I left off my bra and put on a thin shirt.

"I know you remember how we used to fuck and carry on," Don said.

"Yeah, I do, but now I'm the one in control," I said as I walked up to him.

"I can fuck you now and then fuck you tonight."

I lie back on the bed, and said, "Don't tease it if you can't please it."

Don licked my ass the other night, but to have him outright eat my pussy was new, for I was new. He took his time and licked on my pussy. I loved it. It was original as he made love to my pussy with his tongue. He caused a sensation to rise in me like never before, but I wasn't going to let it show.

I could feel my nut coming as he buried his head deeper into my pussy and sucked on my lips. I was mesmerized and under a spell. My body shook lightly, for I was holding back and allowed him to eat the sweet taste from my body. When he finished, I said, "Is that all you got because that didn't fade me?"

"I was sure the way you were responding to my tongue that you came," he said.

"The body is a marvelous thing and if you think you can handle the new me, you better think again for tonight, I promise I will have you wanting me and not Pandora, or any other," I said as I wiped my pussy and put a mini-skirt.

"Damn, I see you're different," Don spoke with amusement.

"Different isn't the word, it's new and improved," I replied as I went outside to sit under the tree, and he went down the road.

"What took you so long to come outside?" Party asked.

"I couldn't decide on what to wear."

"You still not drinking either?"

"Nope, no drinking, I'm on some more shit," I said.

"Sounds like you are trying to take my place," Party replied, looking happy.

"You snooze, you lose," I said with laughter.

"You are wild as fuck."

"You girl's hungry? I cooked before I go stay with Pan at the hospital," Aunt Tee said.

"I don't know about Hog, but I am starved the fuck out," Party said.

"Yeah, I'm hungry, too," I said.

We went inside and ate Rotel. I ate like I had never tasted it before. Party and I ate a lot of the dip and chips. It reminded me not to ever fuck on an empty stomach again and I remembered eating that at a birthday many years ago, but the details were sketchy, so I dismissed it.

"You remember something?" Party said.

"I remember eating this at a birthday many years ago," I said as I wiped my mouth.

"You did. We were at Ice's house and her mom cooked it. We also had chips, square sandwiches, cookies, Kool-Aid, and ice cream," Party said as she wiped her mouth off.

"Come on, let us go back outside and sit under the tree," I said.

Chapter 11

We went back outside. A car pulled in and it was Aunt Doll. I smiled my charming smile, and Party said under her breath, "What the fuck she want?"

"It doesn't matter. She's good, but who is that with her?" I asked.

"You act like you don't know him," Party said.

"I don't remember him, how about that," I said, for he was almost ugly looking.

"That is Skeet, her new man since your mama has Don and all," Party explained.

"He must have cash?"

"Yes, he gets a disability check on the first and a fat ass Social Security check on the third," Party said as Skeet went inside Aunt Doll's house.

"Hey girls. How you doing, Hog?" Aunt Doll said.

"I'm great, and how are you?" I asked.

I'm happy for the first time in a long time," she replied.

"That's good to hear," Party said as she handed Aunt Doll a beer.

"Your mama still going to stay with Pan tonight?" Aunt

Doll asked Party.

"She said she was. Right now, she is waiting on a ride," Party said.

"We may take her since I want to see Pan, anyway."

Skeet walked out the house and spoke to us. I winked to see if he was down, and like all the other no-good sons of bitches, he was. I showed him my tongue ring and he smiled. Quietly he said, "Doll, I need to go to the bathroom. Somebody is in the one in the house."

"Skeet, these are my nieces, Party and Hog," Aunt Doll said.

"I know Tee's daughter, but I don't know her," he said.

"She's Pan's daughter. She doesn't get out much," Aunt Doll replied while looking at me.

"Nice to see you ladies," he said.

"Nice to see you, too," I said, but Party didn't say anything. "I'll take him to our house, if it's okay with you," I offered.

"Thanks, Hog. And you better behave," Aunt Doll threatened.

As he and I walked to our mobile home, I asked without turning my head, "You get down, right?"

He smiled, cut his eye at me, and whispered, "Yeah,

what you got in mind?"

"For a big face, I'll suck you quick and guarantee you will nut," I spoke.

"Why should I give you a big face when I have a mouthpiece at home to do it for free?" he replied with a smirk on his ugly face.

"Because my mouthpiece is a hot piece, and I guarantee you will be craving more than my mouth. You'll forget all about Aunt Doll," I boasted.

"Ain't no mouthpiece ever done that. I don't believe you," he said as I made it to the doorstep.

"Give me the money and you'll see," I said as I opened the door and went in first.

Soon as we walked in, I locked the door, and he put the money on the end of the couch. He lay back on the couch and speedily went to work. I had to bypass the piss smell of his pubic hair and sweaty balls. With only a few minutes to get that nut out, he held back but it mattered not.

"Damn, girl, this is so good," he said as his body became rigid.

I didn't say a word, I continued to please him. He came just like I thought he would. With his dick sticking to his leg, he sat up as I took my money off the couch.

"You give bad ass head" he said weakly.

"I know. The next time you get to sample the young ass, too, for the one seven five," I said as I wiped my face off.

"Shit, be here on the first and third of March. I'll get rid of Doll because if your ass is as hot as your mouth, I'm your new customer," he smiled while rubbing his big stomach.

Making a smacking sound with my mouth, I walked out the door. Aunt Doll said, "What's Skeet doing?"

"He was still in the bathroom. I got tired of waiting and left him in there," I spoke.

"Okay," she said as she turned back around and began drinking.

I looked at them all. Sitting around the damn tree, I thought, *men will give them the money they need by talking them out of it. You have to do more with your mouthpiece than spit game, bitches.* I gave more attention to Aunt Doll and how she thought she had a nice man. *Stinking dick bastard*, I thought with a chuckle as I walked closer to them.

"What's funny?" Party asked as I sat down.

"Had a funny thought about something," I replied.

The Gutta Sluts had made it to our yard, and they were, in actuality, some cool ass, freaky bitches. It wasn't any shame in their game because they got down and would let you drink up some of the profits they made. *Dumb fucks, there isn't a day in Hell that I would let bullshit ass people drink up profits that I worked hard to obtain.*

"It's time for Skeet and me to leave," Aunt Doll said while looking at Pinky and Yogi walking up.

"Hog, you, okay?" Aunt Doll continued.

"Yeah, why wouldn't I be?" I asked.

"You seem distant," she said.

"She been distant since you hit her ass in the head and gave her a bad concussion," Party spoke with a little anger.

Aunt Doll looked over at Party, and Party spoke, "What? Did I lie?"

"I'm good, Aunt Doll. In fact, I want to thank you," I said modestly.

"Thank me? Hitting my niece on the head hardly deserves a thank you," Aunt Doll said.

"It does, Aunt Doll, because now I can see clearly about the way things work in the hood," I replied with a devilish look on my face.

"Damn, maybe I should have done that a long time ago," Party said.

"Maybe," I said, and we all laughed.

"It was good seeing you, Aunt Doll. See you both later," I continued as Skeet walked up. I smiled at him and walked off.

Aunt Tee got in the car with Aunt Doll and Skeet. It was

weird how I didn't remember him at all, but his face made me think that I did know him.

"Party, who is Skeet, anyway?" I asked her.

"He's the Gutta Sluts uncle from Hunter Ridge," Party said.

"So, they all change men like that?" I spoke.

"Technically, they never had their uncle, I wouldn't doubt if they tried it," Party joked.

"Oh, okay. They all cool now?" I asked.

"I'm beginning to think you have changed, Hog. You don't seem like the same bitch I used to roll with," Party sadly spoke.

"No, I'm still me, but with improvement," I said as the Gutta Sluts walked up.

Yogi spoke, "Shit, ain't nothing wrong with improving yourself."

We all laughed, but Party continued to stare at me differently. I paid her no attention because I really didn't give a damn what she thought. Cousin Po Boy rode by to head out and blew his horn. I didn't wave, but Party did along with the Gutta Sluts. She let us all know who she had been fucking. *Gullible bitch*, I thought. I never knew her game was weak as shit until I decided to be the bitch the run the hood.

"I'll be back. I have to walk down the road," Party said as she got up to leave.

"Want me to walk with you?" I asked her nicely as if I didn't know.

"Yeah, come on. We have to walk fast," she said as we got up and walked toward Old Jackson.

"Where we going?" I asked her.

"Come ride with me while I fuck Cousin Po Boy for sixty. I'll ask him to throw you a little change for being the cover up," Party said.

"Sure, but I'll ask him myself, I'm not scared."

"Naw, naw, you may try to take my shit," Party said.

"You love him?" I asked her.

"I love the money, and his sex isn't too bad. He's married, but I don't have some type of feelings for him."

"Maybe he is like a sugar daddy you never had, but with dick and money," I said as I smiled.

"Yeah, that could be it, but he is slightly older and like I said, our married cousin," Party said.

I couldn't say anything else because we had made it to Cousin Po Boy's Hummer. He looked at me in a surprising manner and I flicked my tongue ring at him behind Party's back. He shook his head and smiled, all while talking to Party.

"Come on, Hog," Party said.

I got in the back behind Party so he could see me in his mirror. Party thought she had it going on, but it was I that he wanted. The entire trip to Newton Hotel right off I-20 was crazy for me. She talked to him, but he was clueless on what she said. When she looked at me, I agreed and commented on what she talked about. I admit that it was sneaky, but it was pulse racing all the same.

When we made it to the hotel, he went in and paid cash for the room. I said to Party, "I'm going to sit out here while you do what it is you do."

"Girl, he never takes long. I'll be out in about an hour," Party said.

Cousin Po Boy came back, and said, "Hog, what you going to do while we are in the room?"

"I'll sit out here in the truck, I guess, or walk across the street to Wendy's," I added.

"Why won't you drive the truck and go to Wal-Mart or something?" he said.

"What? You letting her drive the Hummer? I haven't even drove it yet, but you digging off in my ass," Party spoke while trying to go off on him.

"You'll get your chance one day," he said to her. Party went in the room.

"I wish it was you I have in the room," he said.

"You should have asked me first," I replied.

"Don't worry, I want a repeat and this time, I'll be I the one the wins," he said.

"You need to give me some money, anyway. What you want me to do, go window shopping?" I added.

He laughed and then opened his wallet. He turned his back, and then handed me a small wad of cash.

"It better be a lot."

"I think you will find it a nice amount," he replied.

I started the Hummer, and spoke softly, "Be nice in there. And you better not fuck her like you fuck me."

"She's an easy screw, be back in thirty minutes."

"Why not an hour?" I taunted.

"She's not that good," he said.

Looking at the hotel, Party was looking out the window at us talking. I waved at her, and she waved back, but her face had a pissed off look. Well, I couldn't help she didn't have skills like me. However, I drove off and opened my hand. I saw three one-hundred-dollar bills. I laughed. Deciding not to go to Wal-Mart, I stopped at the gas station for a soda. Waiting for the time to be up, I went back earlier. When I arrived, I saw Party standing outside the room. I pulled up and parked.

"What's wrong?" I asked as I opened the door.

"He couldn't get up. That bastard, all he could do was feel on me," she said as I laughed.

"Seriously?" I said with laughter.

"Girl yeah, I'm glad you back so I can get the hell away from here," Party said as she got in the back of the truck.

"Wait, your man, don't you need to be sitting up front?" I asked her.

"Girl, you ride up there, I don't want to be near him," Party said.

That was what I wanted to hear. I got out and got on the passenger side of the Hummer. He walked out and smiled, "Why you up front?"

"Party is fed up and wants me to ride up here," I honestly said.

He got in and cracked the windows a little. Party lay down in the back of the Hummer and went to sleep. I knew she was sleep because she had a slight snore. I lifted up my mini-skirt and panties as Cousin Po Boy drove. I opened my legs wide and moved closer. I sat close enough for him to play in my pussy and put his finger in his mouth. It was dirty, but I didn't care. Life was all about chances, and everyday living was a chance.

I was calm and, honestly, I didn't know that being a

bitch would feel so fucking good. He got my pussy very wet before I went back to the house to fuck Don. I continued to lie back for a few more minutes until I thought I heard Party moving around. I moved his hand quickly and pulled up my pants.

My mind began to anticipate what the night had in store for me. Cousin Po Boy dropped us off down the road and drove off going God knows where. We walked up the road. I saw Don come from down the road by Cousin Po Boy's house. Party said, "Here come your daddy."

"Yeah, he is your daddy, too," I said with humor. She only looked at me and pretended to mock me with her nose turned up.

"I'm going to go talk to him, okay?" Party asked.

"What? You don't need my permission. He was thought of to be your daddy before he was ever mine," I said as I smiled.

"Funny, Hog," Party said as she got up to go greet Don.

When Don made it to the driveway, Party ran over to him, and they spoke a few words. He laughed out loud. Rabbit walked out the house and sat beside me.

"Where you been?" I asked Rabbit.

"Sleeping, some of us have to work for a living," he said as he laughed. "What she doing?" Rabbit asked.

"Talking to her daddy," I responded.

"You coming to the Valentine's Day party I am having at the Hole?" he asked.

"I thought the police told you no more parties?" I replied with concern.

"It's simple. No alcohol containers seen by the naked eye. It has to be in your cup, besides, it's not open to everybody," Rabbit said.

"How are you going to have a party at the Hole and everybody not show up?" I asked.

"Easy, it's done by invitation only," he said. I looked at him and laughed. He continued, by saying "What? Black people in the hood can't send out invitations?"

"Rabbit, we are in the hood. How many invitations do you plan to have then?" I said as I laughed at his silly idea.

"Word of mouth," Rabbit said.

"For real, there may not be a lot of people there. Oh yeah, I got something to tell you," Rabbit said.

"What?" I asked.

"I want you to meet this guy. They just moved to Steeletown and his sister said he is a good guy, he just needs to meet a good girl," Rabbit said.

"What makes you think I am good?" I questioned

Rabbit.

"You're not a slut and you are smart," Rabbit said.

"Me? Not a slut?" I laughed at Rabbit as he laughed at me.

"You're not like that. At least your name hasn't been ringing in the streets yet," Rabbit said.

Party walked back over to where we were sitting and sat down. "What y'all talking about?" She asked.

"Rabbit says I'm not a slut, so he is going to hook me up with the new guy," I replied.

"It better not be who I think it is," Party said.

"If it is, too damn late. I told him about Hog," Rabbit said.

"Who you talking about first?" Party asked her brother.

"His sister drives the light green BMW with the sunroof, and he drives the black Charger with tinted windows and black outs on the lights," Rabbit said.

"Hell yeah, that's it. I saw him yesterday and I started asking questions on who he is. They kin to the Gutta Sluts grandmother and they just moved down from either South Haven or Lafayette County," Party said.

"Well, too late. I hooked up with his sister and he wants to meet Hog," Rabbit said.

Party begun to pout over dick her nor had I ever had. I didn't know what the fuss was about. I may not be interested in him.

"He isn't your type, anyway," Rabbit said to his sister.

"If he's not my type, I can make him my type," Party replied, being sarcastic.

"Hello, I am sitting here," I said in a teasing state.

"Well, do you want to meet him or not this Saturday?" Rabbit asked.

"He can meet Party. I don't cry over spilled milk" I spoke as I got up.

"Damn, Hog, you cold," Rabbit said.

"Well damn, Hog if it's like that, you go ahead and meet him. He wants to meet you, anyway," Party spoke.

"Bitch, you're the one that sounds desperate, not me. I don't give a fuck," I replied harshly.

"Desperate?" Party spoke as she turned up her nose. I didn't care anymore, friend or no friend.

"That's what I said, bitch."

"I ain't fucking desperate bitch."

"I'm not so fucking sure about that. You ass is crying over dick that you haven't even had."

I spoke as I got up by saying, "I'm just saying you see a need, fill a need. To me you in need of new men; by all means."

Chapter 12

Pandora came home and Don was excited because she told him that she was having a boy. I just looked at his pitiful, cheating, no good ass. His happiness about having a son was genuine, but that was it. Maybe it was just me. I didn't understand how a man said he loved someone and then cheated on her.

Fuck this love men claim they have for women. Here is my first love right here, I thought as I counted my paper and hid it back in the tin can in the floor of my room.

"Where did all this come from?" I couldn't remember. I shrugged it off and got up. I opened my room door and closed it behind me as I walked up the hall. "Good for you having a boy and all," I said.

"Mahogany, you are still my daughter," Pan said.

"Don't remind me," I harshly spoke as I walked out the door and straight to the tree.

"Party, come on out," I yelled toward her room as I sat down under the tree to relax.

"Yeah, bitch, give me a few," she answered as she stuck her head out the window.

She came outside and we sat under the tree. She didn't seem happy and I knew that something was up, so to be a compassionate friend, I asked, "What's wrong? Why the long face?"

"I've been thinking about you and how you have changed. It scares me," Party sincerely spoke while putting her head down.

"How is that making you feel bad? You're the bitch that doesn't have feelings. You're the girl I've known all my life, you have no heart. So, what's up now?"

"You down, but I feel you have some secrecy about you. I can't put my finger on it, but you are not quite the same. You are loud and kind of devious, to be honest. I'm still ya girl and love you like a sister but let me in on this shit you are doing," Party said.

"Party," I said sweetly, "There isn't anything to be in on that you yourself isn't already doing. I just don't drink or smoke anymore. My mind is on bigger fish to fry and not on just getting drunk like I used to. That shit has gotten old," I said to her with compassion.

"Yeah, you right. It's just me making sure my girl is coming back around," Party said.

"You're all in shit that you shouldn't have any concern. Now, tell me all about last night," I said to change the subject.

"Girl, his ass couldn't get up. He was lying on the bed and when I took off my clothes he said, "You not going to strip tease me for me?"

I smirked on the inside because I knew he was implying to when I strip teased for him the other day. "Go on, girl, and stop pausing," I spoke.

"I have never strip teased for him, so why now? Anyway, I took off my clothes and he was blank. I touched his dick, and it was as soft as cotton," Party explained.

I couldn't contain my laughter. "Serious? Soft as cotton?" I mocked her.

"Not just cotton, but like a cotton pillow. He couldn't do anything but look and touch it. You talking about a pissed off bitch, I was she. This has never happened to us before. Usually when we get to the hotel, we are good and it is awesome, but last night I couldn't believe I wasted my time on him like that," Party said.

"Well, be like that sometimes," I replied.

"Yeah, and to make it bad, he only paid me forty," Party said.

"Well, he didn't have to pay you that," I said.

"Like it was my fault that he couldn't get up. What the fuck?" Party said. We laughed as Party said, "Girl, I have to step up my game. There might be someone else he's fucking."

"You know he has a wife, right?" I said to her.

"No, he said she doesn't want to be a freak, that is why he gets with me," Party said.

"Well, find out who the other woman is, or, better yet, ask him," I suggested, knowing that the other woman was me and probably five other bitches.

"It's not that serious. He is only someone to pass the time until the real deal comes along," she replied as she lifted the half of bottle of gin to her lips.

"Shit let's just lay back and enjoy the day. Forget about dicks and tricks," I spoke as we sat back and let the wind blow on us.

"Who the hell is that pulling up like that?" Party asked as Bone got out the car.

"Hey, whores," Bone boasted with laughter.

"I'm not a whore like you. Whores get laid, bitches get paid. So, that classifies me as a bitch," I joked.

Quietly, just loud enough for me to hear, Party said, "I'm one. I'm a natural born whore" I looked at her and we laughed.

"Where Mama?" Bone said.

"She's on Hunter Ridge with Aunt Doll and Skeet, why," Party asked.

"I come to get some clothes," Bone said.

"Are you moving out?" she asked.

"Just staying a little longer with a friend. Why you

asking questions? You act like the damn police," Bone said.

"The Hill's been quiet without you around here talking outside your neck," Party said.

"Well, I have been laying low. Too much shit been popping off up here and I don't have time to put my foot off in somebody's ass or kill one of these bitches," Bone said as looked serious.

"Do what you got to do, just don't forget that the Hill is your home. Don't be a stranger," I said to him.

"That's good to hear you say that Hog. Party, can you go get my blue duffel bag out my side of the room. I hope Rabbit didn't lock the door again."

Once Party left, Bone said, "Little Cuz, I love you like a sister, but I hear you the shit in the hood. Is that true?" Bone asked as he searched my face for some type of truth.

"I don't have any idea of what you are talking about. I plan to get out and leave the hood. I need a new ball field to play in," I lied dead in his face.

"I hear you're the bad bitch and motherfuckers are waiting for a chance to get some of you. Don't make me fuck somebody up for fucking off with you," Bone said.

"I can handle mine but know this I'm going to get that paper because the love of money moves shit in the hood. Without it, you might as well be dead," I passionately replied.

"You right about that, make those motherfuckers wear a hat. I hear these hoods are ate up with that package and its motherfuckers that have it that you would least expect," Bone said.

"Who is that?"

"Oh, a little bitch I'm fucking from the other side of Newton down Hwy. 15," Bone replied with much excitement.

"Her ride is clean as hell," I spoke as I eyed her car.

"Keep your head off dicks and on books, and you will have the same thing. Don't let any dick feel, that he can make or break you. If you are out here like the street says, don't be out here fucking for free. Get your weight up, stack it up, and make them wrap it up, ya hear me?" Bone said.

"That's what's up. I'm already ahead of you. I definitely won't fuck for free," I said as we hugged.

"Here you go, Bone," Party spoke as she walked up to us and threw Bone the duffel bag.

He let go of me and grabbed his bag out of the air. Party sat back down, and Bone stated, "Tell Mama that I'll be back for the party Saturday with my little friend. We are kicking it at her crib until then."

Bone walked off and got into his friend's car. We sat there stunned at the car as they drove off.

"What was that fool talking about?" Party asked.

"To get our paper up so we can have a nice ride and watch who we sleep with because that package is running wild like fire. Have you heard anything about that?" I asked.

"I almost always use a rubber. Bitches ain't going up in me raw. What about you?"

I knew Party was lying, she must have forgotten who she was talking to.

"I haven't use rubbers in a minute. Guess I call myself trusting a nigga," I said.

"Well, trust or not, he has to suit up. Shit, I love me," Party replied with a very serious look on her face. We sat outside for hours, chilling and enjoying the day as real friends.

The week of school had gone by so fast. Already, Rabbit's Valentine's Day party had come, and I was clueless as to what to wear. It really didn't matter, for I was going to be naked by the end of the night, anyway. It was Friday, and people were getting all kinds of flowers and gifts from their boyfriend or girlfriend. I didn't care about getting anything, but Party did.

Aunt Tee had sent her some balloons and candy. I was happy for her, but at one p.m. I got a shock. They called me to the office and there I saw a room full of roses, balloons, and candy of all sorts just for me. I was overwhelmed with shock. They had to call me because there were too many for me to carry around all day.

I checked the cards. Two were from Pandora and Don, but the rest said:

To: You From: Me. I already knew who it was from. I didn't know that I had meant so much, clearly that one day adventure paid off. I went back to class and the buzz was already around school that men had sent me things.

"Who sent you all those gifts?" Party asked.

"Don't know, they all read to you from me."

"Girl, who did you fuck? Does he have a brother?" Party said as she smiled.

"Girl, I'm not on that shit. Have you seen the guy Rabbit was telling us about?" I asked Party.

"Yeah, seems like all the bitches in this small 1A school all his nuts, but they better get the fuck back because I've been chatting with him and he's coming over to see me," Party said.

"Good for you girl. I'll be there late because I have a meeting with the senior teachers about my grades."

"What could they want? You are very smart and have done a good comeback."

"It doesn't matter, I can handle whatever they have to say," I replied with no concern.

The bell rang and Party headed to the next class, but it was study hall for me, and I didn't have to get up. I went to the bathroom and freshened up. As I entered the classroom and sat back down, I heard the deep voice of a male.

"What's up, chick?"

I turned around to a fine ass nigga standing there smelling good and looking fine ass fuck. His appeal was geeky, but smooth. His hair had waves and his eyes were blue. I had never seen a blue-eyed nigga before. He wasn't that masculine, but his chest was big enough for me to rest my head.

Smiling, I replied, "What's up with you rolling up on me like that?"

He laughed, and stated, "Are you as funny as you are smart?" He squatted by my desk.

"Is the desk behind you taken?"

"It's taken if you sit in it."

He laughed, and replied, "I like your attitude and after meeting you, Mahogany Jeffers, I really like you."

"How do you know my name? I don't recall giving you my name," I said as I leaned closer to him while smelling him on the sly.

"Your cousin, Rabbit, is messing around with my sister, Quita," he said.

"Oh, okay. What is your name? I remember him telling Party and I about you, but didn't tell us your name," I said.

"What did he tell you?" he asked.

"Nothing at all, what did he tell you about me?" I asked.

"He said you are more of my type, and he is right. Out of all the girls here, I really like you more," he said as he looked so suave.

"Well, I am not the girl for you. The old me would have been, but the new me is a motherfucker and you can't fuck off with fuckers and don't get hurt," I said nicely.

"Mahogany, I hear you are nothing nice," he spoke as he rubbed his hands over his lips.

Leaning closer, I said as I stared at him in his eyes, "You can hear the wind, but can you see it?"

Smiling, he shook his head, and said, "No, you can't, but if you were the wind I can definitely see you."

"Have a seat, little man. You're not in my league," I joked.

"I want you and will give you what you ask. Just one night and I promise you will crave me like a sweet tooth craves candy," he replied as he sat in the desk behind me.

"I'm scared of you," I said to taunt him.

He leaned up close to me to almost touch my lips with his, and replied, "You better be because I'll make you fall in love. I got that fiyah."

"Yeah, right. If that was the case, you wouldn't be here trying to get me. Where your girl at?" I asked.

"I'm staring at her right now," he replied.

"Anyway, nigga, Rabbit is having a party Saturday night, meet me there. Unless you are scared of little ole me," I joked, licking me lips.

"I won't just meet you there, I will beat you there," he whispered in my ear.

He nibbled on my ear a little and a sensation of chills went over me. I had to swallow and move my feet because I was losing my toughness. Turning around, I spoke, "My girl Party likes you, so you better get to know her. She might be more of your speed than I am."

He leaned up, and started kissing on the same ear lightly as he said, "What makes you think I won't have her and be fucking you?"

The teacher walked in, and we had to be quiet. I was stunned because I thought Rabbit said that nigga was good. I didn't fucking think so. *Perfect*, I thought. *He will fit in wonderfully, but don't quite know how.*

That class period steamed by and there I was waiting after class with another boy. The teachers had told me I had to be there, and I didn't know what to think. I made up my work and I had been getting good grades, and for them to want to see me irritated me. The teachers walked in, and the Creative

Writing teacher spoke, "You both are curious as to why you are here, aren't you?" He and I nodded our heads, for we had no idea. "One of you will be Valedictorian and the other will be Salutatorian, depends on your report card at mid- terms."

I knew I was smart, but that was beyond my imagination. Me? A girl from the hood with a brain like a suburban kid; made me smile all over.

"Again, we want to congratulate you both for achieving high marks. Mahogany, you have come back to school and stunned all of us. I am so proud of you," the teacher boasted.

The teacher left out and the guy hugged me. His touch was firm, but very gentle. As I put my head in his chest, my imagination began to run wild. I could get used to the fine ass nigga by my side. Immediately, I pushed him back and shook that shit off. What the fuck was I doing?

I didn't know that nigga and he still hadn't told me his name. We stared at each other for a second and I walked off. I had to get away from him. He made me feel funny and I didn't like that. As I exit the classroom, I thought about getting Valedictorian or Salutatorian. Either one I got; it was still good. Walking down the hall, I saw the coach.

He was ready to take me home with his wife in the truck along with my flowers. When we arrived, Billy Goat Hill was silent until Uncle Willie came out of Party's house, and said, "What dumb, old bastard has given you flowers?"

"It wasn't you, so come help get them out the truck," I

said.

Uncle Willie helped me put the flowers in the living room. I thanked the coach and his wife as they left. Party saw the truck and ran over, trying to be nosy. She looked around the living room, and spoke, "Dang, I heard it was a lot of flowers, but to see it is another thing. Bitch do tell. Who gave you these flowers?"

"Don't know, but whoever it is, they should have given me the money. Flowers die, Benjamin's multiply," I said as I giggled like a small schoolgirl.

"What you going to do with all those flowers?" Party asked.

"Give them out to the people in the community. Since it is after five, people just getting off from work," I said.

"How are we going to do that? We don't have a ride. You can just throw them in the garbage," Party replied.

"That's crazy, bitch, I'm not throwing them away. I rather give them to other people."

"Damn, you have changed. And, I think for the worst," she joked.

"Whatever. Let us take them outside and put them under the tree. We will stop people and give them out, how about that?" I suggested.

"Sounds good to me but it seems like I really don't have

a choice" she frowned.

As we took the flowers out and placed them under the tree, we started flagging down people and giving them away. From where we were under the tree, we saw Cousin Po Boy getting in his Hummer.

"I'm going to go in the house, stop him, and see if he'll take one. I don't have shit to say to him."

Party ran in the house, and I flagged Cousin Po Boy down. He joked, "You like the flowers enough to give them out? I didn't know you had a heart."

"You sent a lot. You should have given me the money, I could have used that, but thank you," I said, not knowing if he sent them or not.

"I got all that for a special lady. You know that you have me crazy about you. I can't focus since that day you blew my mind. When can I see you again?"

"Oh, really? I thought I was leftovers," I said with a smile.

"I need to see you again. I got to have you again, Hog. Just say when and I'll be there or to pick you up or something. You got me running around here like a teenager," he said huskily.

"Shush, take the flowers and the next time I stop you, have that green stuff I like. As for seeing you again, I'll get at you about that," I said seductively.

He took the flowers, and spoke, "I'll be back through in an hour or two, and I will have your money."

"Good, we talking green, my favorite color," I said as I laughed.

He drove off and Party walked outside looking pissed. "What was the long conversation about?"

"He wondered who gave me the flowers and why was I giving them away," I lied.

"What he say about me?" Party asked.

"Nothing, he was too busy being nosy," I honestly replied.

"We only have five bunches left. What are we going to do with them?" Party asked.

"One for you and your mom, one for Pandora, one for Aunt Doll, and I guess I will keep one for myself," I said.

"That'll work," Party replied as she took the flowers in her house.

When she walked back outside, I told her, "I met that boy today that Rabbit talked about."

"What boy?"

"The one from Steeletown with the black Dodge Charger. The brother of the sister Rabbit goes with," I said.

"Oh, him, you mean Maine?" Party replied with excitement.

"Maine?" I said unsurely.

"His name is Jermaine Ross, Maine for short."

"He is a whore. That nigga ain't no good," I said plainly.

"Girl, like we not," Party said.

"You do it for pleasure. I do it for money to get out. I'm not trying to make this a career," I replied.

"It's not pleasure all the time."

"Fuck no. Not for me. I'm trying to stack my paper to get out the hood. I have other plans," I spoke.

"Really? And, I guess those plans don't include me," she asked.

"Anyway, I told him you like him, and he needs to get at you because he is not on my level," I continued, hoping she didn't ask me the question again.

"Girl, no you didn't, what did he say?" Party asked.

"He said, what makes you think that I won't holler at her and be fucking you all at the same time,'" I repeated.

"Girl, if he hollers at me, he's gonna fuck me, not you, because I will be good enough," Party said with confidence as she laughed.

"So, you're not into sharing a nigga now? I just might fuck him," I spoke with no regret.

I looked at the showboat bitch. She thought her pussy was that good. I wanted to laugh at her because I had the cake that proved mine was the shit. I looked at her and smiled to say, "I'm not saying your pussy isn't good, but mine is better. I got that fiyah," Party said with laughter.

"I don't want him but because you do want him, you can have him. I was just telling you what he said."

"Who doesn't want him? Are you blind? He is worth trying to get; besides, he would want me first, anyway," Party spoke.

Not letting my anger show because she was really pissing me off with her lame ass pussy, I politely set the competition to my friend, "The day I fuck him, I'll let him get you and compare the pussy, deal?"

"Cool with me, but I'm going to win," Party laughed, and so did I to keep from jacking her tired ass up.

"I'm about to go home. I will see you tomorrow night," I said to Party as I got up.

"Why not tomorrow?" Party asked.

"I'm going to be strategically planning the kill," I replied with seriousness.

"Strategic, what? Girl, stop with the big words. You are

not that smart," Party replied.

"I'm past smart. I'm a fucking genius. I'll see you tomorrow. And, have your game face on," I spoke.

"Tomorrow morning, I'll be at the 35 Quick-Stop Store with Bone, then we going to Wal-Mart, and then who knows where. It may just be tomorrow night when I get back at you," Party replied without a smile.

"Bet that up," I spoke as I was about to leave, for I forgot all about Cousin Po Boy. I assumed he lied, anyway.

Party got up and went in her house, and I went in mine. I showered and was about to get in bed until I heard a light tapping on my back window. I looked outside and it was Cousin Po Boy. I smiled because he did come. He risked us getting busted. I opened my window, and he used the bucket to climb in. He kissed me passionately as he spoke, "I told you I'll be back."

"What are you doing? Don't you know someone could have seen you come up here? People are always out in the hood," I spoke as I looked out the window, hoping nobody saw him.

"I'm to the point where I don't care," he said as he handed me a stack of one-hundred-dollar bills.

Chapter 13

I looked at the money. It looked like a couple thousand dollars. "What is all this for?" I said with glee.

"It's for you. I have always admired you from a distance and now since I have sampled your honey, it's all for you," he said as he shook his head sexually. "I don't have any children and it's all my money. I can do what I want, and I want to give this to you," he continued.

"What I have to do for it?" I asked as if I already didn't know.

"Just love me when I need you to and from the looks of it, I need it a lot," he said.

I put the money under a shirt I had on my desk, and spoke, "I can handle that. Just don't be running around this bitch acting like a jealous, lovesick motherfucker."

I kissed him. I don't kiss any man, but that nigga just dropped me a couple thousands. I could get used to getting his paper. Seconds later, I pulled away from him and closed the window and curtain. I knew Pandora and Don were sleeping next door, so I whispered, "Be very quiet, and hope you took your medicine."

"With you, I don't need it. Just to sniff that pussy keeps my dick hard" he laughed.

He placed his hands under my night shirt and lightly raised it over my head. I lifted my arms to help him and while my hands were in the air, his warm mouth discovered my luscious breasts. I actually got wet from his touch. I figured it was because I hadn't had an orgasm in a while and the touch, I got from Maine was a sign. I allowed his mouth to caress my huge nipples. I couldn't believe I was thinking about that nigga at a time like this.

His tongued flickered back and forth, causing arousal to occur inside of me. I liked the feeling he gave me. I didn't want to, but I pulled away from the sensation and lay on my fluffy, full-sized bed. He pulled off his shirt and it looked like he had been working out, for his muscles appeared larger than before.

"I have anticipated this moment of loving you since the last time I had you," he whispered as he was fully undressed and walked toward me.

He got in the bed, and I replied, "It's your money, have your way with me."

He got on his back and I knew what he wanted. I hadn't done that in a while, but I climbed on top of him and put my pussy in his face, and his dick was all in my face. Slowly, I began to taste him. The slower I went, the more heated the sex act became. On the other hand, Cousin Po Boy was in haste. I had to pull my pussy up from him to let him know he was going too fast, but he had a tight grip on my thighs.

"I can't help it if I'm in a hurry with you. I said you

make me feel like a teenager," he joked.

I dropped my ass back to him and let him give my pussy a tongue bath. *This is feeling damn good*, I thought as my tongue played ring around on his dick head. I pulled myself up whispered, "It's time for me to fuck you. I just hope you don't have a heart attack on this pussy."

"No, Mahogany. It's time for me to fuck you," he spoke with deep breaths.

I lay on my back with my eyes opened as he straddled me. When he lifted up and tilted his huge dick inside me, he closed his eyes as if he was savoring the moment. I felt like I was about to panic because if felt like he had grown a full four inches, but I knew that was highly impossible. His dick was thicker and felt heavier as he pushed it deeper inside me.

I was reluctant to do it, but my pussy had a mind on her own. The bitch became extremely wet as his dick massaged the tight, pink walls. In and out like peek-a-boo, his dick was winning at the game. The more I tried to escape, the deeper he entered me. He was more demanding and more in a rush. He rolled his ass like I was his hoola hoop, and he would grind me harder if he thought I was falling off him.

Working me like a gymnast in search for the gold medal, Cousin Po Boy rocked my body to music that he must have heard in his head. Countless sessions of fucking had not prepared me for the round I fought in that night. He obviously knew what he had come to do and he was doing it well.

By now, sweat was dripping onto my mouth from his moist body, and he was still not letting me go. I knew it was odd, but my body was relaxed and enjoying the ride. I continued to look at him as he was so engrossed with fucking the hell out of me.

One stroke, two fast strokes, and three quick, deep strokes, and then he grabbed the head of my bed, clinched his mouth shut, and buried his nut deep very deep inside me while my nut spilled all over him. If you could see from the ceiling, you would not be able to see me pinned under him. Gasping for breath, he opened his eyes, and spoke, "I have never had a woman to make me nut the way you do. I'm taking a chance by walking up the road to fuck you. It crazy and I can't explain."

I knew how he felt, for I loved the thrill of being caught and the suspense of being an undercover lover to men all through the hoods.

"I don't want to get up off this pussy," he whispered in my ear.

"Then don't. Get hard and let me ride one last time," I tempted him.

"Wipe me off and let me rest," he replied as he frowned when his dick came out of me.

"No, you rest at home and if you want to rest with me, buy me a home. I can't risk us getting caught. I'm already in violation because you are married," I said.

Lying on his back, he cut his eyes toward me, and said, "Mahogany, that ain't shit to me, you must not know just how much money I have."

"I don't care about that, you getting grade A pussy and not just that, its' quality grade A pussy," I boasted as I got up and wiped him off.

"The pussy is immaculate, I ain't kidding about that," he highly spoke.

"What about Party and you?" I asked.

"There ain't nothing to tell. I couldn't get up because I wanted your pussy and your mouth, not hers. She can't fuck me like you do."

"She's not good?"

"Honestly, she's okay, but she acts like a novice. If you put the two of you side by side you would think that she runs shit, but she fucks like she's drunk. I need Grade A."

I snickered because it was funny. I never would have of thought of Party couldn't fuck right. *Well, she does drink a lot*, I thought, and drinking messed with your libido. "Enough talking about her, are we going to fuck again or not?" I asked because I couldn't let him whip me like that and get away with it.

"As much as I want to be here with you, I can't. I have to get back," Cousin Po Boy said as he got up to put on his clothes.

I almost hated to see him go, but I did want to get some sleep before the day broke. He put on his clothes and left out the same way he came in. Soon as I shut the window closed, a knock was heard at my door.

"Who is it?" I asked.

"It's me, Don. I thought I heard voices," he slowly spoke.

"Go back to sleep. There isn't anybody here," I replied.

He began to whisper, "Don't let me catch that motherfucker in here fucking you."

I got up and opened the door.

"You scared you can't get this pussy again?"

"If your mama wasn't half awake, I'd torture that pussy," he threatened as he reached under my gown, stuck his index finger in my wet pussy, and put it to his lips.

"Come on in and get a real taste of this Grade A, then you tell me if you can just walk away from it." I invited him in.

I look down and his dick was rock hard. In our familiar position, he picked me up and slid me on his hard dick. I saw the way he seemed to melt when our bodies came into contact, for he almost dropped me. Knowing I had him where I wanted him, I jumped up and down on him. He fell against my bed before landing on the floor. I began riding him and making his dick reach for me.

He was about to cum when I got up, and instructed; "Now leave, I'm tired of playing games with you. Aren't I supposed to be your daughter? What a damn shame, you dirty dog."

Agitated and half crazed with wanting to get his rocks off, Don just laid there with his eyes wide open. Before he could say anything, Pan called out for him. He acted like he was hitting the floor with his fist, for he was angry because he was ready to nut.

Smiling, I opened the door, and I waved bye-bye as Don left. I finally wiped off and got in the bed. *Why can't leave I leave Don's alone and why I always let him get the pussy when I don't want him to?* I was a lost call, that nigga was supposed to be my so-called daddy.

I lay there staring at the wall feeling nothing. Suddenly, I remembered the money. I got up and counted my stacks. Cousin Po Boy gave me five thousand dollars. I giggled to myself with great happiness. I put it with the rest of my hidden cash. I got back in bed and went to sleep. I truly believed more of Cousin Po Boy's money was going to get me out of there for sure.

"Wake up, Hog," Pan said through my locked bedroom door.

"I'm woke, what is it?" I said grouchily.

"I hate to wake you, but Don and I are going away tonight for Valentine's Day. We might swing by Rabbit's party before staying at a hotel tonight. I don't want you or anybody else to ruin my night with my man," she spoke.

I didn't give a fuck because I fuck her dick just as much as she does, so I asked, "And you woke me up for what?"

"To see if you wanted to ride with us. We are going out to eat dinner at Penn's Fish House," she spoke. Why is she trying to be a mother now? I practically had to raise myself.

"No, I don't want to go anywhere with you two. I'm going to stay here and chill. I'll see you later on tonight. I guess you two trying to play one big happy family," I yelled at her through the locked door as I woke up.

"Okay, okay. You don't have to act like an ass," Pan yelled back as I heard her footsteps walk away from my door.

Seeing that it was later in the day, I got up. I didn't know I slept all day. *Cousin Po Boy must have worked this ass overtime*; I thought as I got up and looked out the window. Pan and Don were leaving, and I was home alone. I saw Aunt Tee Walk outside and say something to them, and she went back inside. I got up and went to shower. Those two disgusted me.

I looked at my wardrobe and didn't see anything worth wearing for the Valentine's Day party at the Hole. I did have to choose something because buying something new was out. I had the money, but I was being Scrooge because those bitches could smell money a mile away.

Leeches is what they are, I thought as I looked through

my clothes some more. After looking in my closet, I decided to lie around the house. A few people hung out under the tree. I was very surprised not to see Party. I wondered what that bitch was up to. It was getting dark, and I was ready to party. *Its Valentine's, why not stand out like a bitch dipped in Kool-Aid?*

I thought as I picked out white laced bra and panty set, a red mini skirt, a red laced see through shirt, and red flats. I added a red and white ribbon in my brown hair. I looked in the mirror and loved the sight. For an added touch, I sprayed Sex in The City perfume in all the hidden spots because I knew it was going to be on, I just didn't know with whom.

Looking and smelling good, I walked out the house feeling fly. Before I could make it to the driveway, Maine drove up. He rolled his window down, and I just looked at him and shook my head. He smiled, and said, "You looking damn good, Mahogany. You need a ride down to the Hole?"

"You can't handle my ride, so I'd rather walk," I responded.

He started laughing as he lay back in the car. "Alright, you are funny and l love a girl with a sense of humor."

"I've already told you that I am not the girl for you, Party is. She is more your speed," I said as the wind blew a gentle breeze, and a piece of my ribbon fell against my face.

"All games aside, you are very beautiful, you know. I would love to take you out and spend some money on you. So, would you go out with me?"

I looked at him and he was serious. He looked so innocent, but so did bulldogs until you quit petting them. I responded quickly, "Why not my girl Party? You know the one I was telling you about the first day we met?"

"And I told you that it is you I am interested in, not her, but I see you are so destined to throw me off her. Where she at?"

"She'll be at the party tonight."

"I know she will, but remember the entire time I am with her, I want you," Maine said.

"I'm trying to get out the way so she can have you, but thanks for the invite," I said as I walked off to go down the road.

"Tonight, save me a dance," Maine said as he smiled and drove off.

"Wait up," I heard someone say. I looked to my right, and it was Yogi. She was dressed up and looking good, except for the cigarette hanging out her mouth and a pint of gin her hand. "Who was that?" she asked.

"This nigga named Maine, he's been trying to roll up on me," I responded.

"He looks like the boy from Steeletown. They just moved here a couple of months ago."

"Yeah, that's him. How you know?" I asked her as we

walked down the road.

"Girl who don't know him. He is so fucking fine, and his ride is sweet. I wouldn't mind getting a piece of that, but we kin" Yogi said as we walked on.

"How you know all this, and you don't go anywhere?" I asked her.

"I go across the highway sometimes. My aunt lives over there and, plus, they stay a house over from her. Shit, I want him but from what I hear, he doesn't get down like that. Niggas in the hood thinks he's gay."

"Gay?" I repeated.

"Yeah, because they are throwing so much pussy at him and he's turning it down."

"I think you are misinformed. He seems to be down-right whore and for him to say that he can have Party and sleep with me, what does that say to you?" I questioned her.

"Yeah, it does seem like he will get down, but shit, I'll get down with him if he let me," she said as she threw the gin bottle in the ditch.

"Well, I'm not interested in games. I have stuff to do and playing games isn't one of them," I responded as we passed Uncle Willie's house.

"I heard Don your daddy?" she asked.

"Yeah, that's what the blood test says, but he hasn't been. But you know how that goes," I said nicely.

"You plan on leaving the club alone tonight?" Yogi asked me.

"Dressed like this? What do you think?" I said as I struck her a pose.

She started laughing and so did I. When we walked through the gates and up the half-paved gravel road, we saw people lined up and the place actually looked really nice. She bumped me, and said, "Hog, here he comes, introduce me."

"Introduce yourself, he's your peeps" I said with an attitude.

Before Yogi could introduce herself, he said, "Mahogany, you ready to give me that dance?"

"It's not dark enough for me."

He started laughing. "I'm sorry, I was trying to grab this beautiful lady before other guys here come and snatch her up." He kept his eyes on me while rubbing my hair.

"She's good, I'm her neighbor, and yo kin folk" Yogi interrupted.

"Excuse me but I don't mean to be rude but Mahogany, please, come dance with me. I'm not taking no for an answer," Maine said as he grabbed my hand and led me to the dance area.

"Fine, one dance, then stop bugging me," I said.

We made it to the dance floor, and he twirled me in his arms. He smelled good and he held me just right. I was blown away by the nice treatment. He didn't try to feel on me or anything he was really being a gentleman.

"You have done a three sixty," I said.

"What do you mean? I'm a gentleman. Always have and always will be," Maine said as he held me closer.

"You come off as a player, and then you act so sweet like you really want me to be your girl," I said as I leaned closer to rest my head on his chest.

"It's not that, it's just that I had wanted you since I saw you. Niggas just pointed me in all the wrong directions," Maine said.

"I just met you in school," I replied, trying to search his eyes.

"Yeah, and you can tell your type when you meet them, too," he said.

"What is your type?"

"You are," he spoke.

We danced and talked for a long time. I did not realize how fast time went by. After all the booty bumping and slow grinding, one couldn't help but to have sex cross their mind.

Point blank, Maine asked, "Cut the small talk. You going to fuck me tonight or what? No pussy, no convo,"

"Let's go fuck. I want to shut you up, anyway. If your dick doesn't stay hard, I will be sure to pass it along the hood." I smiled but was very serious.

We looked around and people were everywhere. I didn't see Yogi, Party, or Ice. I knew it was early, and they liked to make an entrance, so I dipped out with Maine. He was parked in the back of the field. When we got to his car, I got in the back. I didn't know the Charger had that much room, but it did. He got naked and so did I. He opened the back driver side door and smiled as he saw me laying there with my legs open.

"I don't eat pussy, at least not on the first night, but yours does look good," he remarked.

"Hold up. I want to see what I am getting. You might be one of those short brotha's," I said.

He laughed, backed out the back seat, and stood up. I saw a huge dick. It was at least five inches on hard, long, hairy, and ready. His mushroom cap looked over ripe and full bloom. I wasn't sure if I could handle it, but then again, I handled Don's hook. "You strapping up?"

"Don't worry, I always strap up," he said as he pulled out the Trojan platinum condom.

"Before you strap up, hold that pose," I said.

While he stood in the doorway with his spread his legs, I

scooted over to him and sat between his legs. I rubbed his dick, placed the condom in my mouth as I put it on for him. He mumbled, "Damn, girl, you took me by surprise."

I stroked him up and down with my pierced tongue. He moaned and held on to the roof of the car as I continued to pull him to me with my mouth. Every inch of him was in my mouth and down my throat. I couldn't believe that I could deep throat a dick that long, but I did. Almost choking, I backed off and mobbed on the head. He shook and sweat from him, even though it is I that was doing all the work.

Sucking on his golden balls was a delight. They, by themselves, were huge and hung like plums from a thick vine. I enjoyed myself with the newfound treat placed before me. I was memorized because he was about to blow just by me blowing him. I stopped, and said, "If you nut, I'll have to get you up again to fuck."

"Don't stop, I'm about to shoot this nut all in your fucking face."

"So, you think," I said as I went slower to increase the blood flow to his dick. Being a bitch expert, I knew that if there was an increase in the blood, he'd have an erection. I made up my mind to do something different just to see how the results would be.

Getting heavier into my role of sucking his dick, I pulled on him more earnestly. He rocked his body to my mouth as if he was dancing to the music. I went along with it and shook his dick every which way in my mouth, and that was all I needed to do. He grabbed the top of the car and went stiff. Seconds later, all his semen began to fill the tip of the condom. I didn't let go, I slowed down and watched it fill on up. He stood there froze, and he fell back away from my mouth.

Maine walked around the car naked. He looked at me and walked around the car some more. I already knew. I just wanted him to confirm it. He made it back to me.

"Wow, you have a damn bad ass mouthpiece. No one has ever made me walk around to get my thoughts together. Mahogany, I almost forgot where I was. Damn, girl, I'm in love."

"Nigga, stop playing. Now, since the first nut is out the way, you ready to fuck or what?" I questioned.

"Let me get the feeling back in my legs first, shit. And you made my nut fill the top. Shit, I'll hit you in the damn mouth if you take another dick in there," Maine said as he pulled off the used condom.

One night and already he was possessive. I replied, "Well, what you think? I'm single and can suck and fuck anybody I choose."

"I'll be damned. That shit stops now. You're mine. You can talk to who you want, but you better not fuck. I'm so fucking serious," Maine demanded.

"Maine, you haven't fucked me yet. Just wait until I

drop this pussy on you. You'll be head over heels in love," I said as I laughed.

"If your fucking is anything like your sucking, I already know what the deal is."

"What about me? Don't I have some say so?"

"I won't fuck unless you say so," he said.

"Shit. You don't want me to fuck or suck, then the same goes to you. Talk all you want, but eating and fucking is out," I demanded of him.

"I haven't eaten you yet," Maine said.

"Not yet, nigga, but you will taste this pussy," I remarked as I saw that he was getting hard again.

"Just the thought of pulling on me gets me turned on" he pulled out the condom and put it on.

"Wait, sit down and let me ride," I stated.

"Okay, but for now, I will do the drilling."

Maine sat down in the back seat, and I got on top of him. He was hard and I could feel my heart beating in my pussy with nervousness and anticipation. When I first went up, he smashed me back down and took over the sex. I could barely move because he threw me off rhythm and kept me off key.

"Wait. Who's fucking who here?" I asked.

"You trying to fuck me, but I'm trying to fuck you," was all he said.

As he started back fucking me with a lot of power behind his up stroke, we were in tune and the dick was good. He held my thighs every time I rose up and rolled it around. He kicked the seat trying to keep up with me. He even let go of my thighs to hold me around the waist as if I was his lover.

I had a grip on his neck as well because he was unlike the older men I had been used to fucking, he was different. When he held me tight, he didn't let anything come between us, for we both yelled out in pleasure as sweat dripped off my face onto his head. We heard a weird sound as I sat there with him still inside me.

Chapter 14

Feeling that something was wrong, I decided to get off him quickly and when I did semen went everywhere. The condom broke. I looked at him, and he said as he looked down at the plastic ring around his dick, "Shit! This has never happened to me before. What the hell happened? You're not pregnant, are you?" Maine asked, hysterical.

I laughed before saying, "What the hell? Not this early, silly."

"I have never nutted in a girl before. Am I the only one you fucking, tell me now?" Maine asked.

"Too much information. That is a question you should have asked before I fucked you," I said as I got up and wiped off with a towel he put in the back of the car.

I put on my clothes, and he was still sitting there looking stupid. It was funny to me because for him to act so hard, he was acting like a pussy. I was about to walk off and go back to the party, when he said, "Don't have me to pull your ass off the dance floor with another nigga. If don't believe me, try me." I looked at him and laughed because I was going to see if he meant what he said.

Soon as I made it back to the party, Yogi walked over to me, and asked, "Girl, where you been?"

"I was sitting down out of everybody's way, waiting on

Party and Ice to come," I lied.

"They just made it. They have been looking for you," she said.

She showed me where they were, and I made it over to them. "What took y'all so long?"

"Got to make sure I'm on point," Ice replied, looking like a fool.

"Bitch don't play. You know we like to make an entrance," Party said.

"Well, the party is almost over," I said.

"Have you seen Maine?" Party asked.

"Yeah, he was over there," I said as I pointed to him standing by some other guys from across town.

"Where?" Ice said.

Yogi pointed, and I said, "Don't point."

"Shit, I didn't know. I was just showing her where he was," she said.

"Damn, he's fine as hell," Ice said.

"Hell yeah, and Hog thinks she can get the dick before me," Party said.

"She already fucked him," Yogi jumped in.

"What?" Party responded quickly.

"She's high, she doesn't know what she's talking about," I said while looking at Yogi with that bitch, close your fucking mouth look.

"You better not have fucked that dick before me," Party threatened.

"Party, I can get that dick and work it better than you, hands down."

They all laughed, and Party replied, "We already betted, let's see who he talks to first."

"He may talk to you first, but I bet he'll come to me first ready to fuck."

"Hog, you are not a threat to me, I am the bad bitch in the hood," Party shouted.

"Wait one damn minute, I'm a bad motherfucker myself," Yogi spoke.

"Yeah, Party, she and her sister are pretty bad," I agreed.

Another hour passed and Maine kept watching me. I pretended that I wasn't looking and did things to see if he was looking, and he was.

"I've been waiting on him to come over here and he hasn't. I'm going over there," Party said as she took another drink of her fifth cup of vodka and Coke.

"Wait. Let's get on the floor and dance," Ice said.

Sounds good to me," Yogi interrupted as she raised her cup and went to the floor.

We were on the floor grinding and showing off when some other guys came over and started dancing with us. At first, I didn't know what to think because it all happened so fast. Maine came over, and said, "Didn't I tell you not to dance with anyone?" I ignored him and kept rolling my ass on the guy. Without saying another word, he snatched my lace shirt and pulled me off the dance floor.

Party and my girls stopped dancing and came over to us. Party said, "What the fuck you trying to pull by taking her off the floor like that?"

He didn't answer her. He kept his focus on me, as he spoke, "Sit your ass down before I knock your ass down."

Smiling, I said, "Goodbye, Maine. You need to stop tripping."

I walked off and he came over to me. "You think it's funny? Dance again and watch to see what the hell I'll do."

"Why are you acting like this? We just friends. Shit, I just met you," I said.

"Friends?" he said as he looked at me.

"Hog, you need our help?" Ice said.

"No, I got this," I said as I looked at him. Using my index finger, I beckoned him to come near. He leaned closer, and I said, "You can't be possessive over pussy you've only fucked once, remember?"

He looked over at Party, and said, "I don't give a fuck. You can dance, but no more of that nasty shit. You can dance with your girls, but not with another nigga."

We were about to leave when Maine called Party over to him. I looked at him with a devilish look on my face. The nigga was trying to fuck us both after all that shit, he talked. Well, I definitely wouldn't let him play me weak. Two could play that game. They were talking and were about to walk out, but before he could leave with her, Ice flagged him down. He stopped, and she said, "We came here together, we leave here together."

Party replied, "It's cool, he's only taking me home."

They drove off and left Ice standing there. We stayed there about another three hours before the party actually ended. My mind was all over the place. How in the hell was he going to take her home when she lived there on the Hill with us? I couldn't wait to see that lying ass nigga again.

"Y'all need a ride up the road?" Ice asked me and Yogi.

We got in and left. When she dropped me off; Maine was not there, and Party was sleep under the tree. We woke her up and she went in the house. She didn't say a word, only walked off from us. We all looked at each other and dipped. I went in the house and washed off, got in the bed, and a knock was heard at the front door.

I opened it and it was Maine. "What's up?"

"I thought you were gone fucking Party."

"I was, but I had to come hold you. I just can't get you out of my mind," he said.

I didn't turn him away. He came in and lay down in the bed with me. He didn't want to fuck. We fell asleep with his arms around me. The next three weeks flew by. I made Salutatorian and felt so honored because keeping up with books and all the fucking was starting to wear me down.

Maine made eye contact with me and that meant we'd fuck later on, which was almost every other day. Party noticed that when Maine left her house, he would holler at me. She assumed because I hooked them up that he was just talking to me, but the truth was he was fucking the shit out of me and eating my pussy like a mad man.

I couldn't lie. I began to get hooked on him and the way he made me feel. He acted all thuggish, but alone he was like a sheep led to the slaughter whenever I fucked or sucked him. I was having the time of my life. I fucked who I wanted, whenever I wanted, how I wanted, and, best of all, the paper kept rolling in. I had over twenty thousand dollars stored up. I could leave the Hill and not come back, but I wasn't quite ready yet.

There were still a few things left to do. Party and I

weren't hanging out as much because I had to stay after school for school business and fuck, of course. I didn't see Cousin Po Boy much because he began to stalk me. I wouldn't even walk down the road anymore because he broke his neck just to get see me. He became a hazard, a damn risk to my entire plan. I didn't need him fucking it up, but somehow, I knew things were about to get crazy.

It was almost seven p.m., and I was sitting under the tree with the Gutta Sluts because we were waiting on Party to come back from meeting her probation officer. "Ya hear about ya cousin from down the street?" Pinky said.

"No, what happened?" I asked.

"His wife been following him and she says he is fucking one of us from this way," Yogi said.

"How is that?" I asked.

"She claims about a few weeks ago he walked up the road and disappeared into one of our houses. I told her that I am not fucking her husband, and she needs to find out who is so she can stop pointing the finger at us," Pinky said.

"Wow, what she say?" I asked.

"She just said that she will find out because he has bought a house somewhere and whoever she is, he is caking her pretty good."

"Yeah, I told her that if I had him, she wouldn't have a damn thing, but I am not the one," Pinkie said.

"Who is it?" I asked to pick them for more information.

"We don't know. Shit, we thought you or Party knew," Yogi said.

"I don't mean to change the subject, but where has Bone been? I haven't seen him in a minute," Pinkie said.

"He has some girl down 15. Which reminds me, what happened to the baby you supposed to be carrying?" I spoke.

They both laughed, and Pinkie said, "That baby turned out to be a period."

"I know you already know, Hog, but Party must be in love because the guy that pulled your ass off the floor at the party has her nose wide open," Yogi said.

"That's nice to hear," I replied, not really wanting to hear about Party.

"She talking about going to school and slowing down on her drinking," Pinkie said.

"Damn, for real?" I spoke.

"Hell yeah, you haven't been around much, but lately she has been all wrapped up on him," Yogi said as if she was looking for more information.

"Well, I am glad for her. About time she slowed down," I said.

"Back to Cousin Po Boy's wife, I heard she was talking

about quitting her job just to watch him," Pinkie remarked.

"No dick is worth leaving a job over," Yogi continued.

"Shit, he has the damn paper, fuck a damn job," Pinkie replied.

"Y'all bitches crazy," I said.

"Hog, your ass the one crazy," Yogi spoke.

"How is that?" I asked as I waved at the neighbor that passed by.

"When Maine comes over, he has to come to your house before he leaves, and he stays longer there than he does over here. What the fuck is really going on?" Yogi questioned.

"Nothing, but there you go being nosy. You all up in my business," I said.

"Shit, let a bitch in. I know you breaking the hell out of these motherfuckers. The way they caking you, bitches like me have to practically give away a head job. Not to mention ass," Yogi joked.

"Hell yeah, word is you the bitch we love to hate," Pinkie spoke, looking back at her sister.

"The word is wrong," I said as I played it off.

"Bitch, you and I both know that where there is smoke, there's a fire and bitch you on fire," Yogi replied as we laughed.

"Shit, your ass smart as a motherfucker and you're sneaky, almost a bigger backstabber than we are. The difference is we let you know. We know all about that game you playing," Pinkie mocked.

"Nobody's doing shit like me," I said.

"Shit, how we know that your cousin's husband didn't give you ten grand she says he won't tell her is missing from his account? Pinkie asked.

"If he did, I wouldn't be sitting here talking to you two whores."

"He needs to give it to me, but the bastard won't say a damn thing out of the way to me," Pinkie spoke with a little jealousy.

"Probably because he knows you talk to damn much and too damn loud," Yogi replied to Pinkie.

"It's not that I tell it," Pinkie said, trying to get my attention. She repeated it again, "It's not that I tell it, but men do it."

"Do what?" I said.

"Take you and Party for example. Y'all cool as fuck, right?" Pinkie said.

"For sure, she my bitch," I said.

"Add a guy like Maine to the mix, right?" Pinkie said.

"Right. Go on, bitch," I said.

"He'll fuck you and her because if he fucks one of you the other one will tell it, so if he fucks you both, that way y'all don't have shit to talk about," Pinkie said.

"That shit ain't right, but it's tight as a motherfucker. I been there and done that. Pinkie and I both have been in this game long enough that we could write a damn book about this hidden shit. But, that Maine, he's a damn man and a good looking one at that, and smells good, too. Shit, he needs to hit this pussy." Yogi laughed.

"Bitch, you have too many other dicks coming in and out of that pussy as is" Pinkie told her sister.

"You are not the one to talk. You'll fuck our great grandpa if he was alive. You don't have any damn standards. You just suck, suck, and suck. I didn't say fuck because your ass is wore out," Yogi said as she laughed.

"Bitch, you're younger than me, but your pussy walls are too damn weak. A big dick will damn near kill your ass," Pinkie said with humor.

"Settle that shit across the road and down that driveway, you Gutta Bitches. Keep your private talk to a minimum," I said as Cousin Po Boy came through and blew his horn twice.

I played it off by looking at them, but I knew that he'd be coming over later.

"Who the hell he blowing at?" Yogi asked.

"It's me. As if you bitches didn't know that I have a child by him already," Pinkie said.

I glanced at the worn-out bitch and wanted to laugh; knowing that it was hear-say because no blood tests had been taken.

"That is the shit I was talking about. You try to get my ass in trouble. You better hope I'm sober because if I'm gone off that drank, I'll squeal like a damn pig if she asks me. Sister or not, I'm snitching," Yogi threatened.

"You act like you ain't ever had that dick before," Pinkie replied with a little attitude.

"Shit, I'm broke and need some beer. He needs to get this ass today," Yogi said.

"You see, Hog. I keep this bitch near me at all times because she'll get down and I know she'll get down. I got to keep my eye on her. Shit, you and Party don't have that trouble," Pinkie said.

The shit did make sense, but I told Maine he could fuck Party on my terms. The damn Gutta Slut was right. Keep your friends closer than your enemies. Party should have been there to listen to that. Dark was approaching and Party was still gone. The Gutta Sluts and I went home. Ten minutes later, Skeet came over without Aunt Doll.

"How did you leave her?" I asked.

"I told her I was going to go in the Hole for some gin

and beer." I held out my hand, and he said, "Here's your money. I've been waiting on your tight ass all month."

I took him back in my room and I stripped. He got his greasy, sweaty body on top of me. He still reaped of piss and shit. I wanted to throw up, but I needed him to be there when Maine showed up. I held my breath and threw my pussy a few times. Like clockwork, he came and sat beside the bed holding his chest.

"Hog, the pussy too sweet, I'm about to have a diabetic shock." I gave him a nasty look, because I hated that name, but rolled with it anyway, because that's what they do here.

"Take your ass away from here when you do because I don't need shit to tie me to you," I said as I got up.

He put on his clothes, and I said, "The next time you can't bathe before fucking me, don't come. I was in the mood for sucking you for free, but you spoiled it by being stinking."

"Shit, I couldn't bathe. Doll would have known that something was up."

"Get on, I have company coming," I said.

"I thought I was the only one you were fucking?" he remarked.

"Hell no, you're not even my man. I'm just borrowing you once or twice a month."

Soon as he left, I went to shower. I couldn't believe I

stooped that low, but then again, he was a quick client. When I got out the shower, I had on my favorite button up long sleeve shirt, and no panties and bra. I heard a knock at the door. I never asked who was it, I always opened it and when I did, I was shocked to see Cousin Po Boy. Hurriedly, I let him in.

"Why did you come to the front door?" I asked him.

"The coming in and out your window shit is getting old," he said.

"I hear your wife has been asking questions. You need to get the fuck away from here with that shit. I don't need trouble from her," I asked.

"I told her if she goes around asking questions again, she is out. She doesn't have anywhere else to go. I know it and she know it. She told me she doesn't care who I fuck as long as I wear a rubber," he said.

"Do you have a baby down the driveway across from mine? That's the word being told in the hood," I asked.

"It's either mines or my wife's nephew. We both were running a train on her," he said.

"So, what you got up tonight?" I asked.

"I just had to see you. I needed you to know that you are mine. I'm willing to buy you anything I can just to keep you all to myself."

"It's not about me belonging to you because I do fuck

others," I spoke.

"Please, don't say that. You don't know how hard it is for me to already know you're doing it, but to process it in front of me. Please, don't say it again," Cousin Po Boy said, sounding heartbroken.

"Well, tonight I belong to you."

He took off his shoes and came behind me to my room.

"Here," he said. He handed me a piece of paper and a couple more thousand dollars. I opened up the paper and it was a deed to a small house on 21 up toward Sebastopol. My mouth fell opened. "Is this for me?" I asked.

"Yes, it's in your name and I can't touch it. You told me weeks ago that if I want to rest with you to buy you a home; and that's what I had been doing since I left you."

I sat on the bed, and he squat in front of me. He touched my hands, and said, "This we started was as a fling, but it is growing so much more. I want to be with you as much as I can."

"You know I have other friends and one friend in particular who is about my age and really likes me," I said, hoping it was true.

"He may be your age, but he can't provide for you like I can, and he can't taste you like I can."

"I don't know, let me see," I said as I laid back for him.

Chapter 15

With his pants still on, he sucked on the top of my pussy with ease. He was always a gentle lover, but mentioning another seemed to make him harder with his mouth, however, it felt good. Cousin Po Boy ate away on me, and I would occasionally throw my pussy in his mouth. He hung on and held me steady with a firm grip of his hands. Pausing for a second, he said,

"Have an orgasm in my mouth so I can take your sweet taste home with me to smell all night."

Cousin Po Boy began teasing my pussy lips with his massive tongue. He went up and down each side, and nibble in and out the pussy hole. I loved the way he tried to prove that he was the man for me. I didn't mind because since I came on the scene, he hadn't been fucking off with Party. *It doesn't matter, he's caking me*, I thought as I exploded in his mouth for the first time.

He continued to take my pussy in his mouth and suck every ounce of orgasmic fluid that seeped out my lower body. He didn't miss a drop of my love flow, and I didn't care. I was being taken care of by him and by Maine.

"As much as I would love to fuck, I have to go," Cousin Po Boy said.

With a loud clash, he and I both jumped. We ran to the living room and opened the door. Outside, Cousin Po Boy's

Hummer's driver side window was busted.

"What the hell?" Cousin Po Boy said as he ran outside without his shirt on.

I got scared because it could have been his wife, but when I saw the taillights of the car speeding off, I knew who it was. Party came outside, and said, "What the hell is going on?"

"Somebody busted his windows while he was waiting on you," I said.

"Oh, I don't know who did it. Maine just left," she said as she looked at me. She knew he came to see me before he went home.

"Cousin Po Boy, you were looking for me?" Party asked.

He looked at me, and said, "Yeah, I was, but I have to go now. Fuck whoever did this. I'll be back later to see you, Party," he said as he got in his truck and went home.

"Was he really here to see me or was he in there fucking you?" Party asked.

"There is no shame in my game, but he wasn't fucking me."

"What has gotten into you, anyway?" Party asked.

"Nothing, I'm just living in a jacked-up world and trying to maintain. Why?"

"Maintain is one thing, but fucking my dick is another."

"Your dick?" I questioned.

"Hell yeah. You have never been known to get down. All of a sudden you are the queen bitch on The Hill. What the fuck has been really going on with you?" Party asked.

"I am?" I questioned her again.

"If you weren't my cousin, I'd fuck you up for fucking behind me. We agreed not to fuck behind each other. Remember, Hog?" Party said.

"Me fucking behind you?" I questioned once more.

"You acting like you're slow when I know better. Our motto was we don't fuck behind the other one or have your ass forgotten that, too, when you got hit in the damn head?" Party repeated as she stood in my face.

"Party, step the fuck back because you are in my space. As for the motto, you got rid of that when you started seeing Maine. This is what the argument is really about. You can't hack it that someone you really want, wants me. Get down or lay the fuck down," I said as I got all up in her face.

"Like I said, if you weren't my cousin and my damn sister, I'd fuck you up, you backstabbing bitch!" Party yelled louder.

"It takes one to know one, I mean, to recognize a better one. You bitch. I mean, you free fucking bitch," I said.

I shoved her and she swung on me. When I ducked, I hit her in the side and we both went rolling on the ground. I didn't know what happened next, but Rabbit came up and tore us a part. He made sure that we didn't do any more damage to our friendship.

"What the hell up with you two?" he yelled at us both.

"Ask that bitch," Party yelled.

"Y'all hear me?" Rabbit said as he looked at us both.

"She started it," we both said like schoolgirls.

"Y'all better than dick, so don't let it break up years of friendship. Plus, y'all bitches are cousins, sisters at that," Rabbit said.

"It wouldn't break us up if she would fuck her own men," Party yelled at Rabbit.

"If she wasn't a damn slut, she might be able to keep her men, drunken pussy bitch," I scowled as I yelled back at her.

I could tell Rabbit wanted to laugh, but he kept it in, and said, "Hog, take your ass home and, Party, you go in the damn house. Y'all cool the fuck off and talk about it in the morning." I didn't say a word. I went in the front door and out the back door. I sat on the back porch, and Rabbit came over, and said, "I knew you would be out here."

"Yeah, when I have a lot on my mind, I come here," I said.

"You know she's crazy about Maine, but Maine is crazy about you," Rabbit said.

"Yeah, but I had him first and he wants to be with me. It is I that keeps pushing him away. He won't leave me alone," I explained.

"I know, but you know my sister. She feels that all the men must want her and only her. She acts like the nice guys can't want someone else," Rabbit said.

"That may be true, but don't I deserve to be happy? Don't I deserve to have someone to love me for me?" I asked.

"Yes, you do, but if anything brings you sadness then it isn't worth it. I'm not saying that Maine isn't, but only you can decide that. I know Party has some fucked up ways, but she is still your girl and you're still her girl," Rabbit said.

"You right, but I remember what Bone said back here when the three of us were out here," I said.

"Huh, Bone giving out advice?" Rabbit said as he laughed.

I laughed also, but replied, "You can't tell your heart who to love so when I do, I talk about it."

"Well, that is true. Above all, I can't tell you what to do, but I do know you still have a heart, use it."

"Sometimes, I don't even know if I even have feelings and it scares me because of the promiscuous stuff I do," I said.

"Well, above everything, don't be second best to no damn body. Let the guy want you for you and not have had any of your friends. Truth is, if I were Maine, I'll keep doing what I'm doing until one of you realizes that you are toys in his hands with strings attached. You know, a puppet," Rabbit explained.

He gave me time to process what he just said. It made sense and I knew that it meant leaving Maine and Cousin Po Boy alone. Now, Cousin Po Boy I could, but Maine, it would be hard because I was beginning to develop mad feelings for him.

"I know leaving Maine would be hard because he's feeling you a lot more than he does Party, but from what I hear, you told him to go out with Party. You told that man to move on and you still telling him to move on, so what the fuck. You shouldn't be mad a Party; you should be mad at your damn self."

"That is because she acted like he didn't want me. Truth is, he in love with me," I said.

"Yes, he is, and guess what?" Rabbit said.

"What?" I asked.

"This is sort of like how Don got passed around in the family. He started out with one, then the other, and then the other, and rest is history. Don't let Maine be the new age Don between you and Party," Rabbit replied.

"Honestly, it's hard. I really like him, and she only

wanted him because you told me about him," I said.

"True, but now you see how your mom and aunts feel about Don. It's not that they want him, it's just that it's hard for them to let him go," Rabbit explained.

"It'll try to leave him alone," I said.

"Or, better yet, let her think you have because he wants you," Rabbit spoke as he walked off. "Tomorrow, you and Party need to talk."

"Ok, if she'll talk to me," I said as I got up and went back in the house.

Before my eyes, Maine was standing in my hallway. Pan and Don were still down at Uncle Willie's house frying fish, so he just took it upon himself to just walk in.

"Who told you to come in here?" I asked as I walked up the hall past him.

"Who told you to fuck in here?" Maine said as he walked behind me.

"You are not even my man. Remember, you fucking Party. So don't come up in this bitch wanting to be my man tonight," I said.

"I am your man. You belong to me."

"What about Party?" I threw in his face.

"What about her? She's the side bitch and you're my

main bitch," Maine said.

"Didn't know I was a bitch, a main bitch at that?" I said to tease him.

"Mahogany, quit playing games with me. I'm not those greasy old men you fucking. I'm young and dangerous," he spoke as he came closer to me.

"Maine, are you fucking Party?" I asked.

"Am I fucking you?" He said.

"Did you fuck her tonight?" I asked.

"Yes, I did, I fucked her ass good tonight. She rolled that ass all on this big dick," he remarked to strike a nerve in me.

"So, you did fuck her?" I asked.

"So, you did fuck him?" he asked me back.

"Yes, I sucked his dick and drank his nut. By the way, it was thicker and sweeter than yours," I mocked as I made taste noises with my mouth.

Maine grabbed me by my neck and slammed me down on the floor. He had anger in his face. I had never been grabbed on or touched in a mean manner. I didn't know what to do. We stared face to face for a few minutes. He let me go, and then I yelled, "Get your damn hands off me and leave!"

"I am not leaving this bitch tonight. Nobody is getting

my pussy tonight. Do you hear me? Nobody else is getting it. I'll fuck your ass up on The Hill. I'll give these fuckers up here something to talk about," Maine threatened as he raised his voice.

"Just like the window you busted. You want Party, not me. Get the fuck out," I yelled.

"Next time, I'll come in this bitch and I'm going to crack his skull open," Maine said very loudly, grabbing me again.

"Do you want Party to hear you? Remember, she lives next door," I said.

"Fuck her. I'm tired of pretending to be all up on her when it's you I'm fucking for real. I don't want her. Never have and never will," he said as he let me go.

I scrambled to my feet saying, "Get the fuck out of here lying. I told you from day one, I fuck who I want and when I want. Don't you?"

"This is not a drill; this is not a game. I'm a mean motherfucker if someone is messing with my shit. I will not sit back and watch you fuck another bastard," he said as he went toward the door.

Before he opened it, he said, "You think I'm lying, fuck that motherfucker that is coming and watch what the hell I do. I'll kill you before another nigga fuck you."

I was almost scared because I had never had a jealous

lover before. I used to think it was cute, but now he was getting out of damn hand. "Maybe we should call it quits, and you do you while I do me," I suggested.

He turned to face me so damn fast; I didn't know what to think. Maine had me against the living room wall and threatened, "I don't quit, and you don't fire. Is that understood?"

I could only buck my eyes and wink them because he had me by my throat. Maine said, "Don't let me hear you talking about quitting me. You belong to me and only me. This is my throat. I will rip that bitch off your body and shove it up your pussy. Don't keep making me jealous. You don't want to see me pissed off."

He let me go to say, "I have never put my hands on a woman but with you, I'm so damn jealous I can't think straight when I see you with another nigga, a beast comes out. Someone inside me just tears out and wants to kill you for hurting me."

I just looked at him as my breathing slowly became normal. He locked the door and began rubbing my bare shoulders. His touch made me forget about his bad temper as he softly spoke, "I'm sorry, Mahogany. Let me make it up to you."

I didn't want to, but my body knew when good dick was near. He lifted me up in the air and carried me back to my room. He laid me on the bed and unbuttoned what was left of the buttons on my shirt. Taking his time, he kissed my breasts tenderly as he strokes them with care. Maine eased his way down to my pussy and began to massage it with his hand.

"Mahogany, this is my pussy, and it will only know me from this day on. I promise to love you and only you," Maine said.

He removed his hands and began tasting my ever so needed pussy. My toes wiggled and I could not imagine my other lovers taking me that way before. Maine took his time to please me with his mouth. I was overwhelmed with pleasure that I didn't think about Party anymore. *Fuck that bitch for playing with my pleasure*, I thought as he took my mind to another dimension.

Lightning flashed in the room and the rain began to beat against the mobile home's roof, but that nature sound was incomparable to the human sounds coming out of my room. Maine made me produce multiple orgasms with his mouth. I only heard that one could die from being over pleased, and that night I felt close to it. Maine finally got up. I scrunched my legs close to my stomach and Maine entered me slowly. I waited on him to plunge deeper, but he didn't, he made me wait.

He spoke, "Mahogany, you belong to me and only me. You feel this?" He started inching himself a little deeper into me. I could feel it and it was blowing me away with wanton for him to go deeper. "This is for you," he said as he went deeper into my soul.

He went up and down, and around and around. He put all those inches deep into my pussy. He found places in my pussy that I never knew existed. He took me on a mythical journey that only he and I could visit. He had taken me out for a jog many times, but that night he took me on a run.

Maine fucked me slow and when he saw that I was catching up with his body rhythm, he took off and left me, making me yearn for him to give me more. My throat was dry and parched from the moaning and screaming he made me do. When he released my body, I could only lay where I was, for I was too weak to move any further. We belonged together.

The entire spring break, I was with Maine. He and I were together more than we used to be. When he left Party, he would come see me. It began not to bother me anymore because I was getting a piece of a man, even though I could have any man I set my sights on. True as that was, Maine made sure his dick blocking worked.

Cousin Po Boy would come by and blow, but I would not be around to give him the signal to come over. When I wasn't in school, I was with Maine, and if I wasn't with him, I would be in the house studying. Maine consumed all my spare time, even Skeet was angry and talking bad about me because I wasn't doing his greasy ass anymore. That meant Aunt Doll found out and all shit hit the fan, but I denied it because Maine was my alibi, for they all knew that Party and I were sharing the same man.

I thought about moving to the house Cousin Po Boy bought for me, but I still couldn't leave the Hill just yet. I wanted to see Maine every time he went to visit Party. I had to keep an eye on that dick, for all types of thoughts were on my mind. I decided to lie down because I got tired of waiting on Maine to leave Party's house. I went in the kitchen and Don was at the table. I really wasn't in the mood, but I could tolerate him for a few minutes.

"Hog, let me spit some game at you," Don spoke. I sat across from him at the table as he said,

"You better get on your grind and leave this bullshit alone."

"What shit you talking about?" I asked.

"Maine. That nigga is nothing but trouble."

"You're just jealous that I am not sleeping with you like I used to," I hurled back at him.

"True, I am. I respect your game, but I like his better," Don said.

"What do you mean?" I asked.

"He has you and Party like I had your mama and your aunts. I could sleep with anyone of them right now and won't be shit said, baby girl. They respect my game but hate my grind."

I sat there for a few minutes because it looked just like that. Don then said casually, "The finale will be which one of you will cry out to him that the little red girl didn't come this month, and then you will see where his heart is truly at. I know what I'm talking about. I went through the same shit with these sisters, but I was in love with your mother first and when you came along and she said you weren't mine, I decided to hurt her, and when I did Party came along. Now Doll, she was not intended to be in the mix, but by chance I met her, and you know the shit we went through. Now, I'm back with my first love, your mama, and shit, the baby she carrying may not even be mine, either."

Don with a small laugh looked at me and said, "If it's not, I'll just be leaving like I do all the other times. Maybe I'll move on out the hood and get off the Hill, but for some damn reason the Hill has a hold on me and leaving theses sisters is hard for me to do. Baby girl, don't let him do to y'all what I did to these sisters, and many other sisters like them."

"Good advice and it makes sense. I'll give it some thought. When Maine comes, tell him I don't feel well, but truthfully, I need to think," I said as I forgot what I came in the kitchen for.

I got up and went to bed. Making a decision on not seeing Maine wasn't a bad one. Don made sense and coming from him, coming from someone that had done to my family what Maine was doing to Party, and I made me really look at what was happening in my life.

Was destroying Party really worth it? I frowned on that thought and went to sleep confused more than ever. I wanted to destroy Party. She always thought she was better than me and the truth be told, I HATED HER. I couldn't stand that bitch.

Chapter 16

I awoke the next morning with mixed emotions. I actually felt like a newer person after my talk with Rabbit. He made sense on a lot of stuff he told me, and I knew that I had to be the bigger person. I knew for a fact that I didn't want Cousin Po Boy, although, his money was a plus. It was Maine I had the problem with, he wouldn't leave me alone.

I got up went to school as usual, and as usual Party ignored me. I didn't mention her name and she didn't mention mine. When we got off the bus, Cousin Po Boy walked over.

"What are you doing? Coming here in broad daylight and I didn't tell you it was okay to come over like this?" I said.

"You have been avoiding me and I need you. Can I have a quickie? Just enough to get the edge off, off then I'm gone," he replied, already undressing.

"What makes you think Pan and Don are not here?" I asked

"Because Don is gone to take Pan to the doctor in Jackson."

"So, you been plotting on times you can catch me alone?"

"Yes, I need you, Hog. Please, say you'll fuck me," Cousin Po Boy begged.

"If I fuck you good, will you leave me alone until I show you my signal when you can come over?" I asked him.

"Anything to have my dick inside you," he spoke.

I went to my room and took off my clothes. He was already undressed and ready for me. He lay down on the bed and I began to taste him slower than ever. He was already moaning before I could come up off the dick. I mingled my tongue around his balls and sucked on them gently like I used to do, but better. I had more experiences since my last encounter with him.

His dick was rock hard and stood at attention. I cut my eyes toward his feet, and his toes were spread like usual, but looked to be more in a strain. I tried to blow his mind by blowing him off and it was working. *Okay, girl, do your thing quick*, I said to my pussy as I got up and squat on top of him. He felt hard inside my pussy and undeniable good. I remembered how he and I used to fuck, and how a skilled lover he could be. I began to fuck the way Don did by fucking him side to side.

He was at a loss for words and so was I. He held my thighs tightly to make sure I didn't come off him and, honestly, I wasn't. I loved the feeling he gave me as his pumps met my pussy. I began to moan and fuck him harder than I normally would. It was a special day because he was getting the special for free.

"Wait, get up and let me take over," he said.

I didn't want to move, but anything that would make

him explode quickly was good to me. We changed positions and when he laid me on my back, he began to lick me and even suck my toes. I was blown away, for Maine, or any lover of mine, had not done that before.

"No man has tasted your toes because they only want to fuck you and not make love to you," he told me as he continued to make my toes wiggle.

He eased back up to my pussy and began tasting her. I wanted to release in his mouth, but if I did that, then I would want him to get the fuck on. I knew he wouldn't leave until he nuts, so I held myself back, and said, "Come on before someone comes and disturbs us."

Taking heed that it was still daylight; he got back on top of me and began pounding my pussy harder than ever. He rough fucked me and that was something I hadn't had in a long time. *He knew I needed it*; I thought as I fucked him back when I could. My pumps back to him were no match for his rough thrusting. He was an animal in the pussy, and she was quietly being beat down by an older warrior.

When he did cum, he was loud, and I was loud with him. Even after his nut, he still tried to hump and pump me, but the dick was getting soft, and I hated it. The dick was worthy, and I actually wanted some more of that rough shit he just gave me. Breathing hard, he said, "I have to go. My wife will be home soon. I'm supposed to take her out and fuck her later, but I had to have you first. Your pussy was calling me to come get it, and I did."

"Yes, you did."

"I know I am not that young stud that has been fucking you lately, but he don't love you and nor can he financially take care of you like I can," he spoke.

"It's not that he can't do it. I just like him for him, that's all."

"Oh, you don't like me for me?" he asked.

"You married. As a matter of fact, cousin," I replied with a little laugh.

"It's not like I can stay married," he said.

"Don't leave your wife for me or anybody. It's not worth it."

"Yeah, I know the saying that I'll leave who I'm with for somebody else, right?"

"You know it, so get up before someone sees you."

"You know everybody sees everything here in the hood."

He got up and wiped off. I watched him, for he was not a bad looking man, and his sex is really damn good, almost better than Maine's.

I thought about *Maine*. Just the thought of his name made me smile like I had a pot of gold. He must have seen me smiling hard because he said, "That young dick has you sprung, doesn't he?"

"I'm not sprung, just caught up," I said.

"What does that mean?"

"Never mind, just hurry up and go," I ordered.

Cousin Po Boy eased out the door and I was there alone. About an hour later, I looked out the window and Ice was outside. I went in the down the hall and the door opened. It was Ice.

"What's up, Hog?"

"Nothing, what's up with you?" I questioned back.

"Shit but want to know about you and Party. What's up with this bullshit I hear about you two?" Ice said.

"Don't even mention her name to me," I angrily said as I sat down.

"I would have gotten here sooner, but I was locked up in court session after session. I wasn't allowed to call or see anyone until the trial was over and now that it is, I am here. Tell me about it," Ice said.

"Rabbit wanted to introduce me to Maine, but Party jumped in wanting him. I told her she could have him after I slept with him so he could compare us since she claimed he wouldn't like it."

"Damn, that's fucked up. So, y'all mad over dick? A

lean piece of muscle that comes a dime a dozen. Y'all bitches are cousins, best friends, and sisters. That's sad."

"It's not just that; it's the principle of the fact that she thinks she is better than I am. She has always thought that and I'm so tired of it," I said.

"You know like I know how a bitch can be, so cheer the hell up. Don't let him come between y'all more than he already has. Party is your cousin and best friend. Wake the hell up," Ice truthfully spoke.

"What do you suspect I do? Not be happy?" I asked her.

"I expect better from you than her. Tell me how you feel about Maine?" Ice asked.

"I really like him, but he won't leave me alone. When I did profess that we break it off, he grabbed me and snapped. The makeup sex was worth it," I said as I gave a small laugh.

"The shit's not funny. In my line of work, I have seen firsthand how it starts out innocent, but it turns deadly quickly. Do you love you?" Ice asked.

"You know, I say I do but my actions don't act like I do, don't it?"

"No. To tell you the truth, they are dangerous and unlike you." She got up, and continued, "Come on out here with me. I'll make sure no more licks are passed. Y'all motherfuckers better get on the right path."

"Okay, okay. But, if she starts talking outside her neck, I will lay her down." I got up and closed the door behind us as we walked outside. Party was sitting under the tree. She looked different and she turned her head as she saw that I was with Ice.

"What she doing out here?" Party said.

"She is here because I told her to come. Y'all need to talk and make back up. You know damn well that this shit is wrong. Y'all mad over dick. Get fucking real," Ice spoke harshly.

"I don't work well with other bitches," Party replied with much attitude.

"Neither do I, but I can adapt if the bitch has what I need," I said.

"Shut the fuck up talking to me," Party said.

"Watch ya mouth for I put more than a dick in it," I yelled as Ice stood between us.

"Both of you shut the hell up and let me talk. Hog, you sit on the other side of me while I sit in the middle between you two bitches. Y'all won't fight today." Once I was seated, Ice spoke, "The problem is Maine, right?"

"No, the problem is Hog and her slutty ass ways. She has to fuck every dick I fuck, and we swore not to do that," Party reminded.

"The problem is not just me, it's you. You knew I

screwed him first and you didn't care. You always want to be the top bitch, and you can't take it if you are really the runner up, but I showed your ass that you can be the second best on this Hill," I said.

"Runner up? You got to be kidding me. Cousin Po Boy, Skeet, and who the fuck else doesn't count," Party said.

I stood up, and said with fake tears in my eyes, "Party, I have told Maine and the rest of them to leave me alone, but Maine gets violent. I get quiet, but I'll tell you this, anyway. From this day forward, you can have him. I miss being your friend and I miss hanging out with you."

In the back of my mind, I remembered the old saying, "Keep your friends closer than your enemies," and if I have to lie to get back in with Party, I would.

"You mean that?" Party said.

"Yes, if he comes out there to talk, I'll tell him to leave because he is all yours."

"Hog, it means a lot to me to know that you are on my side again."

"It means more to me than you will ever know," I said as I stood up and gave her a hug.

"Thank you, Hog," Party said.

"You are welcome. When he comes today, I'll take him to the trailer and tell him about it. No funny business. You can even be there. What will you do once he turns violent toward me every time, I try to leave him alone?" I said.

"He's violent with you? I wonder why?" she asked.

"Because he says I am his, I belong to him. I've tried to let go and the last time he choked me down."

"Wow. I didn't know all that," she replied.

"Do you want to be right there when I tell him that I can't see him anymore?" I asked.

"No, that's okay. You have never been a big liar, and I know it sounds silly, but I still trust you," Party replied.

"See what talking can do to friends?" Ice added.

"Yeah, it does help, and I missed you, too, Hog" Party said.

"Let us all make a pact not to ever do this again because dick is not more than family. Besides, you two need to stop this shit in your family. Don't let dick break y'all up, too," Ice said.

We all promised and hugged, for that day was a fresh new start on our newfound friendship. We were all smiles and happy again. Then, we heard someone say, "Save room for me."

It was Yogi. She yelled that out as she trotted closer to us. We laughed at her because she was always ghetto, real but funny. Ice spoke, "Hurry up."

She came up and hugged all of us, and said, "It feels

good to know that we are all together again."

"We? When did we three have another number?" Party said.

"Bitch don't play. I may not be your close kin, but shit, I'm family and when something is wrong up here, trust me, something is wrong down there. We feel the effect of bullshit," Yogi replied.

We all sat down in our usual spots. Yogi lit a blunt. Ice hit it and she passed it to me, but I denied it and passed it to Party. Then, Party denied it and passed it back to Yogi.

"Bitch, you didn't hit that. What the fuck is up with you?" Yogi said.

"Nothing, I can't change my habits?" Party said.

"Hell no," Yogi said as she got up and got in Party's face.

Yogi stared at her for a few moments, looking her up and down. She looked at us with a smile, and said, "Bitch, when is the baby due?"

I could have shit sesame seeds out a dry ass. I had to look over at Party and she was just sitting there with a wide ass smile. My heart began to thump out of whack and my senses ran crazy. *How the hell did this happen?* I thought as I held back the tears. "You pregnant?" I asked.

"I haven't seen the little red girl in a few weeks," Party

replied slowly.

I wondered how that could be if he didn't screw bare back. *I will find out;* I said to myself as I sat there looking stupid like Don said I would.

"How did you know?" Ice asked Yogi.

"My sister has enough of them and it's fairly noticeable. You just have to know what you are looking for," Yogi said.

"Party, what you have to say for yourself?" Ice asked.

"Nothing, Maine's gonna take me to the doctor this evening, but he thinks I am going for an Army check up," Party said.

"Bitch, if you joining the Army so will I, and I know damn well I'm not going to fight a damn thing," Yogi said as she laughed.

"Congrats, Party," Ice said.

"I'm excited and nervous all at the same time. Think about it, me a mother, me having a baby by the man that loves me," Party spoke as she looked at me.

I hated the fact that she was rubbing it in my face that she had been fucking Maine as I had. I didn't like it, but if she continued, she was going to pay for bumping her gums about having a baby by Maine.

"Hog, that is why I wanted you to leave him alone

because I had the feeling that I was going to have a baby by Maine. Don't you think he will make a wonderful father?" Party asked me.

I wanted to sucker punch the bitch in her mouth for asking me shit like that about the man I happened to love, too. Sitting back, I knew they all waited on my response, so I said, "Yeah, he'll be a wonderful father to his children."

"What children? I'm carrying his first child," Party said defensively.

"I'm pregnant, too," I replied, not knowing how she was going to take it.

The look on her face was worth all the money I had hidden in my treasure box. I could not have planned such a wonderful outcome. I needed to see if what Don says is right.

"Bitch, you lying," Party said as she jumped up and paced around the tree.

"Hog, if you are joking, it's not funny. Take it back," Ice said.

"This shit is better than any damn T.V. show I could watch right now. Shit, Jerry ain't got shit on Billy Goat Hill," Yogi remarked as she lit her cigarette and opened a can of beer.

"Ice, I am not joking. I'm pregnant," I said as I looked over at Party.

"Hog, why are you doing this to me? Why me? I have

been your best friend," Party said.

"Mine is simple. I have sex to get out of the trap and you have sex to get in a trap. Don't worry; I'm not going to tell my baby daddy. You just don't tell your baby daddy," I said.

"What are you talking about?" Party asked.

"Excuse us," I said as I walked off. Party came behind me.

In the background, I heard Yogi say, "Shit, I want to hear, too. This is just getting good and y'all bitches want to walk off and talk about it like it's going to change something."

"Yogi, be quiet and let them talk," Ice interrupted.

We went into my mobile home, and I closed the door. "What are you talking about, Hog?" Party asked.

"You know like I know that Maine isn't the only dick you fucking, so cut the crap," I said.

"He is, Hog, he really is," Party said.

"I know that you are fucking Cousin Po Boy, and for the last month or so you have been sneaking off to be with him. Tell me I'm lying, and I will shut up."

Party was quiet, before saying, "So what? You can't have it all, Hog. I wanted in on all the dick you've been getting. So, what if I don't get the cake like you? So, what if I give it up freely? So, what if I don't know who the real father is? Let me enjoy being pampered by the man I love."

"Which one? Maine or Cousin Po Boy?" I asked.

"Hog, I love them both," Party said.

"You know you can't love them both. You will care about one more than the other, so which is which?" I asked point blank.

"In all honesty, I love Cousin Po Boy, but I know you care about him to some extinct. However, I care a lot about Maine but that is just it, I care about him," she replied.

"I see, but if you pick one, I will pick the other, and leave the one you pick alone, deal? No more secrets and no more of this going behind the other's back," I spoke.

"How can you decide on who you want to love or not love? There really isn't a way to tell. They both make the perfect man, but my body only craves one of them," Party replied.

"Well, Party choose and choose wisely, for there aren't any do overs or take backs," I said.

"Okay, let me think on it. Maine just pulled up. I'll tell him to come holler at you when we get back. Do you want to hear the news from me or him?" Party asked me.

"From you as long as it's true," I said. Party smiled and closed the door.

It seemed like Party and Maine were never coming back. I had been waiting on pins and needles for them to return, and nothing. Don came in, and said, "What did I tell you?" He paused, and said, "I knew that something like this was going to happen. I could see shit like this unfolding a mile away and, yet you think I am crazy."

"Yeah, you told the truth," I said.

"I heard y'all talking and let me tell you how this is going to play out, baby girl. She's gonna choose him because he's young and has a higher stamina. It's not about love because tricks don't know how to love. They only fuck up those that love them. I already know, but I must say that you aren't pregnant, so let me guess. You're only lying to see to see where his heart is at?" Don said.

"I guess we'll have to see if Pandora's baby comes out to be yours or not. Guess you'll have to see that, too," I replied, trying to hurt his feelings.

"You hard, Hog," Don said as he laughed.

"I never would have thought of you turning out to be a cutthroat bitch. What did Party ever do to you?"

"Don, it's like this, those that can learn, teach, those that can't, learn. Party just happens to be one of those that will never learn," I said.

Don got up to walk toward the front door. He opened it, and said, "Hog, you a bad motherfucker and I respect your game for that."

I went in my room and lay down on the bed. The truth was I don't know if I was pregnant and as much as I would love for it to be Cousin Po Boy's, it wouldn't happen. I would know who the father was, and I couldn't tell him just yet. I had to play my cards right and when the time came, I would feed him a lie that he couldn't refuse to eat.

About two hours later, Party opened the door and walked in. I was sitting there waiting on her. She looked happy and giggly. "I am pregnant and it's Maine's. The baby is due sometime in November."

"Congrats, girl, happy for you," I spoke in a nice and happy tone.

"Yes, it means a lot to me to have you by my side," Party said.

"So, you are sticking with Maine, right?" I asked.

"For sure, I'm really going to get spoiled by him," Party said.

"That is good to hear," I said as I knew she was trying to rub it in my face again. That bitch. "I already told him that if it's a boy, it's going to have his name," Party said with a smile.

I gave her a hug and she opened the door. Before she went out the door, she said, "I'm going to tell Maine to come over, okay? And thank you again, Hog, for stepping back and allowing my child to know its father. It means a lot to me."

I gave her a fake smile and she closed the door. That bitch knew like I knew that Maine wasn't the father, but if she wanted to pull out whore tricks, then I would, too. Maine came over and I was still sitting in the living room. He closed the door and said, "Baby, I know you done heard and I'm so sorry."

"Yeah, I have. What you going to do?" I asked.

"Not a damn thang. She knows it's not my baby like I know," he said.

I laughed, and said, "You still with her?"

"Free ass and they say that pregnant pussy is the best. I'm about to find out," Maine said.

"I thought you never go in a girl raw. Or were you faking that night of the Valentine's Day party?" I asked as I turned my nose up at him.

"I wasn't faking that night at the party. I had never fucked Party raw. You crazy, she fucks everything. You are the only one I fuck bare because if I get something, I know where I got it from."

"I told Party since you and her are about to be parents, I will leave you alone," I said.

"Like hell you did. You're not leaving shit alone. If any damn thing, I will leave her ass alone. I'm not losing you over a slutty bitch," Maine said.

"Well, she isn't a drunk anymore. She is pregnant like I

am," I said.

"You didn't tell me that you were pregnant," Maine said with surprise in his face as he lifted me up.

"I didn't tell you because I'm unsure if it is yours or not because the time, I got pregnant, if I am pregnant, we had just started messing around,"

"When would it be due?"

"October, give or take. Why?" I said.

He was quiet as he said, "At least there is a possibility of it being mine and I can deal with that, I just can't deal with a liar. I'll be alright with her if she would tell me yes, Maine, it may not be yours, but don't come telling me that it is mine and only mine because I know she'll get down."

"What about me and mine, if it's so?" I asked him.

"I'll be almost hurt, but I knew that I wasn't the only one when I met you. In fact, I have been the main one, but I am not the only one. Like that bastard's window I busted out," Maine said.

I laughed, for it was funny now, but not so funny then. I asked, "You still going to be with me or is this our goodbye?"

"Hog, I care a lot about you. I am not leaving you. Like I said earlier, I will leave her before I leave you. I insist that we continue to be together and go from there," Maine said.

"I promised I will leave you alone and I must," I said unconvincingly.

He came over to me, lifted my chin toward his, and kissed my lips lightly.

"You can leave this alone?" he said as he kissed me again.

I puckered up my lips, kissed him lightly back, and said, "Maybe I can try, but I need more convincing that I can't leave you."

He said with a twinkle in his eyes, "Fuck all this talking about her. I'm ready to fuck you, the one I really want to be with."

That was all I needed to hear. I held his hand and led him to Pan's room. It had a huge bed and very soft mattress. When I opened the door, he said, "This is the first."

"It's different because we are different. We may be having a baby, and I am thrilled, no, honored to know that a child is growing inside of me."

"Hog, I'll take you anywhere you want, in the Dodge, in the shed, in Pan's bed, in Party's bed, anywhere as long as I am with you," Maine said, making a joke.

Chapter 17

Before we could get naked, a knock was heard at the door. I looked at him to say, "Put your clothes back on and let us go back up the hall because we are getting disturbed, and I don't like to get disturb."

He looked dumbfounded but understood. We put our clothes on and went back up the hall. He sat on the couch, and I opened the door. It was Cousin Po Boy. I was shocked to see him standing there looking pissed. I stood out the way and let him come in. Maine looked him up and down before saying, "Hog, who the fuck is this?"

"I'm here because I need to talk to Hog," Cousin Po Boy said in a tone that was unlike him.

"Maine, leave us alone for a little bit. I want to see what he wants," I said.

"Yeah, mangy, leave us alone," Cousin Po Boy said.

I quickly turned my head to face him because he talking like that was so not like him. Maine jumped up off the couch and got in Cousin Po Boy's face. I tried to stand between them, but they were standing toe to toe. I fell down and that worked. They stopped trying to get at each other to see what was wrong with me. I had to fake being a little hurt, and I did like a pro. They each wanted to take me to the doctor, but I got up and said, "I just felt faint a little. Please, do not argue. Maine, leave us alone, okay? I'll be fine."

"If you need me, I'll be in the yard under the tree," Maine said.

"Are you really alright?" Cousin Po Boy asked.

"Don't worry about me. Why are you showing up unannounced and trying to throw out my company?" I demanded to know.

"I hear you're pregnant, is it mine?"

"I don't know. You were there and that's all I can tell you for now."

He got on his knees in front of me and placed his head on my stomach. He then rubbed my stomach in a circular motion. He spoke softly, "I hope you are my little one. If so, you and your mama will want for nothing. You hear me, Mahogany? Y'all will want for nothing."

"I hear you, but don't you have a child by Pinkie?" I asked.

"We tested that child last week and it's my nephew's baby. That is why having this child as mine means the world to me."

"I understand, but I can't magically make this child yours," I said as I rubbed the back of his head. Seeing that I had him, I said, "When did you start back sleeping with Party?"

"About two months ago because you were so wrapped up with mangy."

"I want you to stand up, and guess what?" I said.

He stood up, looked down into my eyes, and said, "What?"

"Party is just that far along, and she has a better chance of having your baby than I do," I said.

His look was blank as he frowned and moved away from me. He looked back at me, and said, "She's pregnant, too?"

"Yes, and it may be your baby since you didn't tell me you were screwing her again," I spoke with such distaste.

"It's not like that. I got…"

"Shush, I don't care. Go on and talk to her. From now on, you bring money when you come see me. Don't bring your apologies, don't bring your I forgot, bring me money or stay the hell out my face," I said as I went down the hall.

He came behind me, and said, "What about the house I bought you? What about the money I gave you? What about my love for you? Doesn't all that count for something?"

"Those are extravagant gifts that one buys a lover," I said.

"Hog, are you saying that I mean nothing to you?"

"You mean a lot to me, it's just that you are married,

and you are family," I said.

He cut me off.

"It's not like it's written in stone."

"I know, but you are married and if you really desire children, then go to Party because she is, like I said, more than likely carrying your child than I am. I care about you, but I care about your happiness more," I said as I looked at him.

"You are right, but will I be able to still fuck you?"

"If your money is still green and, who knows, you may get me pregnant one day," I said as I opened the door for him to leave.

"Hog, I love you no matter whose child you carry. If you need anything, give me a holler and I will come running."

"Okay, we'll see if you mean what you say," I said as I closed the door and went to bed crying for no reason at all but hormones.

The sun peeked through the curtains of my window, and I wanted so bad to magically shut them without getting up. Frantically, someone was beating at my bedroom door. I couldn't make out the words, but I opened the door, and it was Don.

"Your mama is going in labor; she's going in labor."

He took off back to their room and I was behind him.

Pan was lying on the bed, squeezing the sheets and moaning in such pain.

"Don, help her up while I go get a ride for us to take her to Lackey," I said as I ran out the door. As luck would have it, Aunt Doll showed up in her truck. I ran to her, and said, "Pan is in labor, and I need you to take her to the doctor."

"Shit, I'll be damned. I'm drunk as hell and I ain't driving a got damn thang. Here, bitch, take the keys and y'all take her. Bring my shit back," Aunt Doll said.

"What is going on?" Party came outside to ask.

"Pan is going in labor," I yelled out.

Don came outside carrying her as I opened the back door for him. "Wait, I'm going," Party said as she hopped in the back with Pandora.

I got in on the passenger side while Don drove with the emergency lights on. We were passing vehicles left and right. We passed the highway Patrol. He threw on his lights, but Don kept on driving crazy.

"Pull over, Don!" I yelled at him.

"If he wants me to pull over, he better catch the tail end of this truck at Lackey's," Don replied as he drove like never before.

I called Lackey Hospital and told them that we would be arriving shortly with a pregnant female who was going into labor with a highway patrolman behind us.

"Why you do that for?" Don asked as we turned off Jones Street onto the hospital street.

"So it won't look like you are deliberately doing this," I said.

Soon as we got to Lackey, it was like a movie scene. Police cars were everywhere and in tow was the highway patrolman. Soon as we opened the doors, he yelled for us to come out slowly. We did and he came up and handcuffed Don. He tried to explain what was going on, but they put him in the back of the car and came over to us. They had to secure the situation before hospital personnel could come near us. Once the area was secured, they came over and got Pan out the car.

Party and I waited for the doctor while Don was still outside with the police. The doctor came out, and said, "Congratulations, it's a boy. We are going to send him and the mother to UMC for further observation."

"Can we see them?" I asked.

"Yes, only for a few moments because they are about to be transported by ambulance. Before she leaves, we need her name and any information you can give. She is not cooperating with the staff," the doctor said.

"Hog, you're a big sister, I'm so happy for you," Party said as we walked down the hall to see Pan and the baby boy.

"Keep him away from me. I don't want to see that damn

baby," we heard Pan yell.

"Ma'am, it's your baby," the nurse said.

"It's a mistake, a damn mistake. He done fucked my life up," Pan spoke harshly.

"Excuse me, nurse, I am her daughter. What is going on?" I asked.

"Your mother doesn't want to see her baby."

"Let me see him," I said.

She handed me my brother, and Party said, "Damn, I see why she doesn't want to see him. He doesn't look like Don at all. He's a white man's baby."

I looked up at Party, for she was right. My little brother didn't resemble Don at all, and I don't have a clue who the daddy could be. I now saw why she didn't want him because Don might have a fit, so to buy some time, I said, "Party, don't let Don come in if the police release him. Don't let him know she has had the baby. I need to think of something."

"Okay, Don and I will take Aunt Doll back her truck. I have to go to court tomorrow to get off house arrest," Party said.

"Okay, get up with Ice and tell her to come to the hospital. Don't tell anyone she has had the baby," I repeated.

The ambulance came and got her and my little brother.

The entire trip in the back, Pan said, "I was so sure it was his, but I forgot about that one time with him."

"With who?" I asked.

"You don't know him."

"Know who?" I asked. She didn't say anything before she continued to cry out of control.

"Pan, whose baby, is it?" I asked her, for I needed to know.

Between tears, Pandora turned her head, and said, "His name is Todd Lair, the man that runs the corner store on 80. I was in need of a high and he gave me what I needed. In return, I had to give him what he needed. Oh, Hog, what have I done? Don will kill me for sure. It's the second time I have done this to him. I didn't know, I swear."

Pan began sobbing more. She cried about Don and how he felt than her own son, me, for that matter. *She did tell me she would have pissed me out too*, I remembered her saying. Bitch will pay for that. We arrived at the hospital, and they transported my little brother to the NICU, and they took Pan to a room. When we got in there, I said, "Sign him over to me and let me raise him. That way, Don won't know. I'll tell him you lost him and signed yourself in a half-way home."

"You'll try to help me? After all I put you through?" Pan said with tears down her cheeks.

"Yes, that's what a loving daughter does," I said so

sweetly that I even bought my own lie.

"I'll do it, but not right now. I can't think straight now," Pandora said.

"Well, you don't have long to think. Tomorrow is the deadline. You can tell them you don't know who the daddy is just so we can't get some temporarily papers going. We need to get you away before Don tries to kill you for being a liar to him. God forbid if he saw the baby, he'll go ballistic," I said, putting emphasis on everything.

I know Don wouldn't do it because he already knew it may not be his. He had his coming when I got back to the hood.

"Hog, you right. What you got in mind?" Pandora asked me.

"Make me his legal guardian while you are away somewhere."

"Where will I go?"

"Mental institute because you tried to kill me."

"How will we do that?"

"After tomorrow, you will see. Let me think some more."

Pandora went to sleep, but I had orders for no one to see her, that way if Don tried come over, he couldn't get in. Ice arrived over and I told her some of my plan because you never let your left hand know what your right hand was doing.

When Pandora woke up, the notary lady was there, and Pandora wrote a statement saying she wants me to be the legal guardian of my brother. She also signed papers for me to have power of attorney over her in case something came up and she was out of her mind.

"Okay, we have signed the papers, how do we get me insane?" Pandora said.

Being it had to be genuine I waited until I saw the security guard coming. I leaned over to her, and said, "Bitch you have been a problem since I could remember. You would always leave me alone and I had to learn about fucking the hard way. Thank you, bitch."

"Hog, what are you talking about?" Pan asked in confusion.

"I haven't stopped fucking Don, even when you told me he was my father. We even fucked countless of times in your bed. Plus, the baby I'm now carrying is Don's," I said with an evil grin on my face.

Once Pan's brain translated what I had said, she came after me and tried to hurt me. I yelled for my life. Although I could have taken her, I needed to feel afraid so the guards would buy it. They came in and tied her down. Pan's actions were real, for she was telling me that she was going to kill me and the baby I carry. Her hurtful words landed her in the East Mississippi Mental Hospital for the mentally insane. I didn't want to do it, but she needed to get away and that was her ticket.

While Pan was being shipped away, I had time to think about the rest of the bastards on The Hill that had grieved me. I took a break and went to see my little brother. I don't intend for him to be caught up in that type of lifestyle. Closing my eyes, I anticipated on what the next day would bring.

All those bitches on Billy Goat Hill would pay. I was going to burn that motherfucker down. My little brother would be in the hospital for a maybe a few weeks or up to a month. He was healthy, but the doctors wanted to make sure that he wasn't addicted to crack or whatever else Pan was on.

Before leaving the hospital, I named him Jermaine Tobias Jeffers. He looked so adorable and cute. I almost hated to leave him, but there were a few loose ends to tie up, starting with my so-called daddy, Don.

When Ice and I arrived to Billy Goat Hill, I looked out the window and there stood Bone and Rabbit throwing up bandanas in the air hollering BGH. They always tried to represent the BGH gang lifestyle.

Oh, they on that gang shit, I thought as I rolled up the window and laughed at my favorite cousins. *How I'm going to miss them.* Party came out the house, then, Aunt Tee and Aunt Doll came to the door. I wasn't in the mood for talking because I had to execute the first piece of my plan, so I went to my house. Soon as I opened the door, Don was standing there.

"I have been waiting on you. Why can't I see Pan or my son?" he asked.

"Truthfully, it is not your son, he's half white and she is terrified of seeing you," I said point blank.

"Not again, first with you and now with him," Don said as I went through the mail.

I saw a letter from University of Southern Mississippi. I opened it and was smiling like a champ. It was my acceptance letter to their design department. Everything was working out like I expected it to. I closed the letter and went down the hall to my room. I closed my door and opened my treasure box.

My deed was still there along with my money. I got the box out and covered the hidden spot back up. Not caring for any clothes, I looked around my room one last time and left out. Soon as I got up the hall, Don was still there. "Why won't you talk to me? Is it because of the father of your child?" he asked as he waited for me to say something.

"Don let's get this straight right now. I love you and if you weren't my father or the father of my baby I would marry you, but I can't," I said.

"You mean the baby you aborted?" I looked at him because I didn't think he knew about it, but he did. "That's right, I knew all along. I didn't know it was mine until you aborted it, and I heard you and Ice talking. I made up my mind to fuck you every chance I got for aborting my baby. Don't get it twisted, the pussy is good and the head you give makes a man do wrong, but I always wanted you with my child," he said as he looked at me.

"Don, congratulations to you. I am pregnant with your child, but the saddest part is that my child won't know you because you are a sicker than a motherfucker. Did you know that you have HIV, and so does Pan, Doll, Tee, and all the rest of the bitches you have fucked got it, including me," I spoke.

"What the fuck did you say?"

"You got HIV, motherfucker. I didn't stutter," I repeated slower to make sure he understood what I was saying. Don sat down on the couch as if the blood drained from his face. He wouldn't look at me. I continued to say, "When I got hurt, I found out you gave me syphilis, gonorrhea and Chlamydia, too. Although, I continued to fuck your good ass dick, I couldn't leave it alone until I found out I was pregnant. It's fucking sad, because you are my father. I don't know who is worse off. How could you fuck your own child and continue to get her with child?"

Don didn't say anything. All he did was sit there.

"I got a letter from the Health Department and my results were positive for the virus. You have to tell everybody you were fucking, you son of a bitch. We all are going to fucking die because of you. Your ass got sick and did not try to figure out what was wrong with you. Instead, you hid it from everybody. Your ass brought this disease to the hood from wherever the hell you came from."

I walked over to the front door and looked back at him. His demeanor was quiet and confused. He glanced up at me. With a bitter heart and pain on my mind, I smiled, and spoke, "Die a slow horrible death, you incest bastard."

I needed him to think that it was his baby so he could die wondering if he had a child or not. I lied about being pregnant, but who gives a fuck? That was his punishment from me, actually, his death wish. Walking out the door, I left him looking like the sick bitch that he was.

I saw my folks outside, so I walked over to Ice, Party, Aunt Doll, and Aunt Tee. I knew what I had to do would be hard, but it was long overdue and much needed.

"How is Pan doing?" Aunt Doll asked.

"You book smart, but a dumb ass, street bitch at real life," I jumped.

"Hog, what the fuck you say?" Aunt Doll said.

"You heard me. You do nothing but let no good motherfuckers use you. That alone tells me that you yourself ain't about shit. You are stupid and for now on, you'll be known to me as a latchkey bitch because you latch onto any man with a hard dick and with little to no income. Bitch, you should have stayed in school and got a real job because the one you on is firing," I said as I turned toward Aunt Tee.

"I should have busted your damn head opened," Aunt Doll said with slurred words as she sat there moving her head from side to side. She was wasted as usual.

"No, bitch, putting me in the hospital was the best thing that has ever happened to me and for that, I really thank you. My eyes became open to the bullshit I lived by. Besides you need to get your ass checked for HIV," I said, facing Aunt Tee again.

"I don't have anything to say about you but leave these tired ass dicks alone in the hood. You have been doing it for years and shit hasn't changed. What makes you think they ever will?" I said.

"Hog, I am surprised at you," Aunt Tee said.

"Don't be because of your daughter and the rest of these sick ass whores think the way I do."

"Bitch, you ain't got anything to say about me. I have always had your back," Party said.

"You always had my back until you started fucking behind my back. Those babies you carry are not Maine's and he knows it like we all know it. They are Cousin Po Boy's. I know the truth and so do you," I said.

"Why are you doing this to me?" Party said.

"Why?" I screamed out. "Because you always had me thinking it was my fucking fault for being smart and when I was your true friend, you made me feel like I was nothing. It took getting hit in the head to see that you're not about shit. You backstabbing whore, you are nothing and you will never be nothing. Hope Cousin Po Boy take your kids because if you raise them the way you raised yourself, they will be jail bound and I would have to pay for them to live in the prison," I remarked.

Ice looked at me, and I said, "Let's go. I've had enough of this shit; it's beginning to make me sick." Before I walked off, I spoke, "All you bitches are supposed to be blood. How? You all fucking the same man and guess what, that silver tongued bastard has given all of us HIV. Yea, bitches, go get your pussy's check. We are going to die around this bitch."

All I got see what their mouths dropping. I was sad about having HIV, too, but those bitches were going to be the saddest. Ice did not say a word. She got up and got in the car.

"Where you going?" Ice asked.

"Take me to a car lot. I have to get a ride so my brother and I can have transportation."

"Where you going to live?"

"I have a place my pussy already paid for," I said as I laughed and waved by to the Yogi and Pinkie, for they were walking to Billy Goat Hill. I yelled out the window, "You two bitches better get checked because Don running around this bitch giving motherfuckers HIV."

They stopped in their tracks, staring at each other as Ice pulled off.

"What about your baby?" Ice asked.

"What baby? I lied about being pregnant. I've learned my lesson. I have an education to get and a brother to watch after. I hope you'll be at home in Jackson because I plan to burn this bitch down.

"What the fuck has gotten into you? Burn The Hill down?"

"Yeah, I'm going to set this bitch on fire soon. I'm going to gather up some gas and put it around their homes. I don't give a fuck who dies. All these bitches can rot in hell. I've gone through a lot here on Billy Goat Hill. My daddy was fucking me. My mama's brother was fucking her. Aunt Tee, Aunt Doll, and Mama were all fucking this disease infested ass Don. I'm tired. Family or no family. I'm burning this bitch down tonight," I broke down to Ice.

"How? People are out all times of night around the hood."

"Girl, please, after I told those bitches they have HIV. The hood will be very quiet tonight. And, you know those Gutta Sluts can't hold water. Those bitches probably have it, too. Shit, I know they have it because Don has had both of them. Trust me, boo, the hood will sleep tonight."

Chapter 18:

Last Stand on Billy Goat Hill

Three months had passed and each day that went by, I awaited the perfect time to return to Billy Goat Hill. I hadn't contacted Party or any of my other close relatives. That kind of bothered me because we all went from being close to being far. I sat there, for I know in my heart that it was not all my fault.

If it hadn't been for Aunt Doll making me fall, I would not have realized just how fucked up I really was and how much I had stood in Party's shadow. I was always the backup girl, the one she kept close, but far.

Bitch, I wished I had this wake-up call sooner, I thought as I thought about my family on the Hill. At last, the time came because there was an upcoming Hill party. Aunt Doll was throwing a big birthday bash for Rabbit. The Hill loved to have the center of attention and if you weren't at the Hill, then something was wrong with you. That was exactly what I needed. I needed everyone to hear what I had to say about my so-called family. It was time to meet the ones that I had waited a long to put in their place.

When I arrived, I sat in the car for a few minutes before Ice said, "You sure you want to do this?" I looked at her as if she had lost her mind. My look must have told her the answer. "No matter what happens, you still my top bitch and if this is what you want, go for it."

Smiling at her, I spoke, "That means a lot to me to hear that from a true family member."

Before I could finish talking, she spoke, "Do what you have to, but, bitch, I don't plan to lose my job over it."

Turning my head toward the crowd of people, I saw that all five of those bitches didn't let the cat out the bag about them having HIV. So, I decided that I was going to be the bearer of bad news. Ice and I did not say anything more. We continued to glare at the many people at the big birthday bash.

Waiting for more people, the party became packed. Everybody drank and smoked dope like always. They had DJ Smooth on the mic. He spins records with all the new shit. Just when everybody was letting loose, I felt their eyes on me as I approached the DJ platform. "What this bitch up to?" someone said.

Still focused on my destination, I grabbed the mic and DJ Smooth turned off the music. People started yelling and shit until they saw my pretty face.

"What's up, kin folks? I know all you motherfuckers didn't expect me here tonight, but I'm here to spread the word. Everybody around this bitch should know me, but if you don't, my name is Hog. I'm Pandora's daughter. And I know you all know Pan. My so-called family banned me from up here on The Hill because I delivered some bad news."

I heard my aunt say, "Somebody get something to shut that bitch up."

However, I continued on talking.

"But, the good thing about that shit is that I don't give a fuck."

As I was about to continue, Aunt Doll, Aunt Tee, Party, Pinkie, Yogi, Bone, and Rabbit ran up in front of the crowd. They all stared at me.

"I see my family has moved to the front of the crowd. Good. Let me start with this nigga on The Hill y'all know as Don. Don supposed to be my daddy, but he fucks me on a regular basis. He got another daughter pregnant, plus, he's fucking all my aunts. How can a sorry, non-working bastard fuck his own fucking kids? That's a sad motherfucker."

The people in the crowd started acting confused and stunned.

"My Aunt Doll is a small female, but dumb when it comes to men. She's still fucking Don, but Don is supposed to be her sister's man. Damn, your own family is dangerous. My Aunt Tee, I love her to death and really don't have shit to say about that. Pinky and Yogi, as you all know as the Gutta Sluts, I love y'all to death, but you bitches need to stop fucking and sucking all these men you don't know about. And, my girl Party, now, this bitch is my cousin, my sister, and my best friend. We all know that she's fucking Cousin Po Boy, Maine, and the rest of you motherfuckers around here. She's pregnant by Cousin Po Boy and said it was Maine's. Bitch, get real."

I was about to continued when Aunt Doll spoke out,

"Don't do this, Mahogany."

"What did you say, Aunt Doll? Don't do this? Do what; tell everyone at this party that you bitches have HIV? Yes, motherfuckers, Doll, Tee, Party, Don, Pinky, Yogi, and plenty more of you bitches have HIV. Y'all still fuck these nasty ass whores. You better go get checked."

"Bitch, tell you got it, too!" Party yelled out.

"You are right, Party. I was fucking behind you bitches and I have HIV, too. I've cried because I grew up to be like the family I never wanted to be like. It's sad because I thought about coming back and burning all these motherfucking houses down because you bitches are nasty. But I'm not going to do that. You know what, I just might. However, it matters not what I do because all you are going to die a slow, poisonous death any damn way. It's sad because these nasty bitches at Billy Goat Hill are infected with HIV. Niggas beware, be fucking aware who you let fuck and suck you for the low low!"

I gave DJ Smooth back the microphone. Even his mouth was wide open, so I figured that meant he is fucking one of them, too. I heard someone say, "I'll be damned if that bitch gave me that shit. I'm going to kill that bitch and I done gave it to my wife, oh Lord."

"Bro, I was just with that bitch last night, hell no!"

"I'm going to cut the fuck up if that whore ass bitch done poisoned me and can't get rid of it!"

The more I walked through the crowd, the people parted like the red sea. I went over to Ice, got the gas, paper, and lighter. Someone in the crowd said, "She 'bout to burn this bitch down. Oh shit, I got to get the hell away from here. Shit, I'm on paper!"

"Crazy ass bitch. What you about to do with that?" Aunt Doll asked as I began to walk toward my old house.

"Bitch, you went to school, figure it out," I spoke harshly as I started dashing gas on the trailer. I felt someone coming; therefore, I turned around and spoke angrily, "Get the fuck back before yo ass burn like this bitch."

"Calm the fuck down, Hog. This is The Hill. This is our home," Bone said to me, slurring.

"Bone, I love you and Rabbit-like brothers, but fuck this," I said as I continued to dash gas on the trailer I grew up in.

Bone turned, and yelled out toward his mom, "Y'all think this sick bitch playing? She for real tonight. You better get off your infected ass and start taking shit out that bitch if you want to have something for tomorrow. I'm about to get the fuck on down because I don't do the law!"

Aunt Tee yelled out, "Everybody, help grab my clothes, get my shit out, this snake body ass whore done lost her damn mind. Help me, help us. Bone, this bitch is striking and biting with her cold ass. I told her mama she was a snake mouth bitch just like her daddy. Now look. She worse than I thought!"

A tear escaped my eye, but I did not let that get to me. Walking fast, I started dashing gas on the fuck shed and lighting it, also.

Aunt Doll said, "Look at this bitch, she fucking up the business. Now how am I going to rebuild?"

My last stand was the house that Party grew up in. No one tried to stop me. They were going fast as they could to take stuff out the house, but not fast enough. I started pouring gas more fiercely and without regards, I lit the paper and the laid it on the gas-stained spot. Instantly, the fire was on way.

Ice stood there waiting on me. We got into the car and drove off. All around, cars pulled out the Hill as if they were on a racetrack. I wanted to destroy Billy Goat Hill because my life was destroyed there.

Epilogue

I lost Maine in the process, but he returned months later after he found out he was infected with HIV, too. Pan was still locked down in the East Mississippi Mental Institution. I moved into the house Cousin Po Boy had bought me with my little brother, Jermaine. Maine and I raised him as our own. I ended up getting pregnant for real by Maine, and we got married.

Ice stopped hanging around The Hill. Don moved away and found a new bitch out of state. And, as for Party, she had twins. Cousin Po Boy and his wife tried to sue for custody of the babies, but Party disappeared. Nobody ever heard from her again.

My plan backfired because motherfuckers were still fucking all those nasty ass bitches on the new Billy Goat Hill. My plan was to destroy them, but nothing happened. Niggas were still lined up trying to fuck.

Billy Goat Hill almost destroyed me, but I learned my lesson. The one thing the HOOD taught me was "To Never Trust Your Motherfucking Family." I threw my hands up and never looked back. DEUCES!